CATE TIERNAN

AWAKENING

The fifth book in the series

PUFFIN BOOKS

PUFFIN BOOKS

Published by the Penguin Group
Penguin Books Ltd, 80 Strand, London WC2R 0RL, England
Penguin Putnam Inc., 375 Hudson Street, New York, New York 10014, USA
Penguin Books Australia Ltd, 250 Camberwell Road, Camberwell, Victoria 3124, Australia
Penguin Books Canada Ltd, 10 Alcorn Avenue, Toronto, Ontario, Canada M4V 3B2
Penguin Books India (P) Ltd, 11 Community Centre, Panchsheel Park, New Delhi – 110 017, India
Penguin Books (NZ) Ltd, Cnr Rosedale and Airborne Roads, Albany, Auckland, New Zealand
Penguin Books (South Africa) (Pty) Ltd, 24 Sturdee Avenue, Rosebank 2196, South Africa

Penguin Books Ltd, Registered Offices: 80 Strand, London WC2R 0RL, England

www.penguin.com

First published in the USA in Puffin Books, a division of Penguin Putnam Books for Young Readers,
2001
Published in Great Britain in Puffin Books 2002
1

Printed in England by Clays Ltd, St Ives plc

British Library Cataloguing in Publication Data
A CIP catalogue record for this book is available from the British Library

ISBN 0–141–31404–4

To GC and EF, with many thanks

1.
Embers

They fled tonight, the lot of them. Selene Belltower, Cal Blaire, Alicia Woodwind, Edwitha of Cair Dal, and more—all slipped through my fingers. They knew I was closing in on them. It's my fault. I was too cautious, too worried about proving the case against them beyond all doubt, and so I left it too long. I've failed, and badly. And worse, Morgan nearly died because I didn't stop them.

I've got to break the warding spells and get into Selene's house. She can't have had time to pack up all her things. Maybe I can find some clue, something to tell me where she went or what her group is planning.

Damn, damn, damn!

—Giomanach

I stood with Bree Warren and Robbie Gurevitch, my two oldest friends, on the lawn in back of Cal Blaire's house. Together we stared at the flames that leapt hungrily up from the pool house and cast a smoky pall over the stark November moon. Somewhere in the inferno there was a crash as a section of the roof caved in. A fountain of white-hot sparks flew skyward.

"My God," Bree said.

Robbie shook his head. "You got out of there just in time."

Sirens wailed in the distance. Though it was the last night of November and snow lay inches deep on the ground, the night air felt hot and dry as I gulped in a deep breath. "You guys saved my life," I managed to choke out. Then I doubled over, coughing. It hurt just to breathe. My throat was raw and my chest ached and every cell in my body craved oxygen.

"Barely," Robbie murmured. He tucked an arm under my elbow, supporting me.

I shuddered. I didn't need Robbie to tell me how close I had come to dying, trapped in the tiny, spell-wrapped room that had been hidden in the pool house. Trapped by Cal Blaire, my boyfriend. My eyes, already stinging from the smoke, blurred again with tears.

Charismatic, confident, inhumanly beautiful, Cal had woken something that had been sleeping inside me for sixteen years. It was Cal who had first loved me, as no boy ever had. It was Cal who had helped me to the realization that I was a blood witch, with powers I'd never even known could exist in the real world. It was Cal who had shown me how love and magick could twine together until it seemed that all the energy in the universe was enfolding me, streaming through me, there for the taking.

And it was Cal who had lied to me, used me. Cal who, less than an hour ago, had tried to kill me by setting the pool house on fire.

The wailing sirens of the fire trucks sounded closer now, and I could see the reflection of their whirling lights faintly in the dense clouds of smoke. The red made a hellish glow against the roiling gray. I turned to see where the trucks were, then gasped as two dark, faceless silhouettes loomed up in front of me.

They resolved into Hunter Niall and his cousin, Sky Eventide, two English witches who'd arrived in our little town a few weeks ago. Oh, right, I realized foggily. I'd sent them a witch message, too, begging them to help me. I'd forgotten.

"Morgan, are you all right?" Hunter asked in his crisp, accented voice. "Do you need a doctor?"

I shook my head. "I think I'm okay." Now that I could breathe, my body was starting to thrum with adrenaline, and I was getting a weird, disconnected feeling.

"There'll be an ambulance coming with the fire trucks," Bree pointed out. "You should let them check you out, Morgan. You inhaled a lot of smoke."

"Actually, if Morgan's up to it, it would be better if we left now." Hunter cast a glance over his shoulder. The first of the fire trucks was turning into the curved gravel driveway in front of the big house where Cal and his mother, Selene Belltower, lived. "I don't think we want to talk to anyone official. Too many awkward questions. Sky, if you wouldn't mind delaying them for a moment so we can make our getaway . . ."

Sky nodded and set off across the lawn at a smooth lope. Stopping a few yards from the house, she held up her hands.

I watched, puzzled, as she moved her fingers in a complicated dance in the air.

"What's she doing?" Robbie asked.

"Casting a glamor," Hunter explained. "She's making the firemen believe the fire has spread to the house. The illusion won't last more than a few moments, but it'll keep them from noticing our cars while we're driving away." He nodded his approval to Sky as she hurried back toward us. "Let's get going. No time to waste. Robbie, if you'll drive Morgan's car, we can all meet down at the end of the block."

I was dimly amazed by the swift way he took charge of the situation. No exclaiming over what had happened. No expressions of shock or horror. Just business. Normally that would have irritated me. But at that moment I felt reassured; safe, almost.

Robbie hurried toward my car. I started to follow him, but Bree took my arm. "Come on, you can ride with me," she said.

My gaze met hers. Even at the scene of a fire, her glossy, shoulder-length hair looked perfect. But the shock of what had happened showed in her dark eyes.

Once we'd been so close that we'd finished each other's sentences. That was before she'd fallen for Cal, before he'd chosen me. This morning Bree and I had been enemies. But tonight I had called her, sent her a witch message with my mind, when I was facing my darkest hour. I had called out to *her*. And she had heard me and had come to my aid. Maybe there was hope for us yet.

"Come on," Bree repeated, and led me toward her BMW. She helped me into the passenger seat, then went around to the driver's side. As we drove down the narrow, winding back driveway, she glanced anxiously in her rearview mirror.

"They're still running around the main house. No one's even gone into the backyard yet," she said. A smile tugged at her lips. "Sky's spell really worked, I guess. All this witchcraft stuff really blows my mind."

She gave me a sideways look. "It was wild hearing your voice so clearly in my mind," she added after a moment. "I thought I was going nuts. But then I figured, enough bizarre things have happened lately that I probably should take this seriously."

"I'm glad you did. You saved me," I replied. My voice was hoarse, and the act of speaking triggered another coughing fit.

"Are you sure you're okay?" Bree asked when I straightened up. "No burns or anything?"

Not on the outside, I thought bleakly. I shook my head. "I'm alive," I said. "Thanks to you." It wasn't exactly a reconciliation, but it was all I could manage at the moment.

At the end of the dark, quiet block we pulled up to the curb behind Sky's green Ford. Robbie was already there, leaning against the door of my car, Das Boot. I winced as I looked at the battered '71 Valiant. It was already dented and missing a headlight from a minor accident I'd had a week ago. Then, moments ago, Robbie had used Das Boot to ram through the wall of the pool house where I was trapped. Now the hood was badly dented, too.

"Right, then," Hunter said. He spoke briskly, but I felt like I was hearing him through a layer of heavy cloth. Somehow I just couldn't focus. "People are going to be asking a lot of questions about what happened here tonight; how the fire started, and so forth. We need to get our stories straight. Robbie, Bree, I think it's best if you simply pretend you weren't here. That way no one will question you."

Robbie folded his arms. "I'm going to tell our friends in Cirrus the truth," he said. "They have a right to know." Cirrus was the coven Cal had started. Robbie and I were members, along with four other people.

"Cirrus," Hunter said. He rubbed his chin thoughtfully. "You're right, they should know. But please, ask them to keep it to themselves." He turned to me. "Morgan, if you can bear it, I need to talk to you. I'll drive you home in your car afterward."

I cringed. Talk? Now?

"Can't it wait until tomorrow?" Bree asked sharply.

"Yeah," Robbie agreed. "Morgan's a mess. No offense, Morgan."

"I'm afraid it can't," Hunter said. His voice was quiet, but there was a final tone in it.

Robbie looked like he was about to argue, but then he simply handed Hunter my car keys.

Sky turned to Hunter. "I'll try to find out where they've gone, as we discussed," she said.

"Right," Hunter agreed. "I'll see you at home later."

"Where who's gone?" I asked. This was all moving too fast for me.

"Cal and Selene," Sky told me. She pushed a hand through her short, silver-blond hair. "Their house is sealed with warding spells, and both their cars are gone."

I swallowed hard. The thought that they were out there,

who knew where, was terrifying. I had a sudden, irrational conviction that they were hiding behind a tree or something equally melodramatic, spying on me at this very moment.

"They're not in Widow's Vale anymore," Hunter said, as if he'd read my mind. "I'm sure of it. I'd be able to tell if they were."

Though the logical part of my brain told me that nothing is ever certain, something in the way Hunter spoke made me believe him. I felt a burst of relief, followed by a wash of intense pain. Cal was gone. I'd never see him again.

Hunter put one hand under my elbow and steered me over to my car. He opened the passenger door, and I slid in. The inside of the car was frigid and that, combined with the adrenaline still pumping through my body, made me shake so hard, my muscles started to ache. Hunter cranked the engine, flipped on the one remaining headlight, then pulled out onto the quiet, tree-lined street.

He didn't say anything, and I was grateful. Usually Hunter and I were like sparks and gunpowder. He was a Seeker, sent by the International Council of Witches to investigate Cal and Selene for misuse of magick. He'd told me they were evil. Before I'd learned, to my horror and shock, that he was right, Cal and I had almost killed him. That was just one of the things that made me intensely uneasy around him.

In one of those weird connections that seemed common among blood witches, Hunter was Cal's half brother. But where Cal was dark, Hunter was fair, with sunlight-colored hair, clear green eyes, and sculpted cheekbones. He was beautiful, but in an entirely different way than Cal. Hunter was cool, like air or water. Cal smoldered. He was earth and fire.

Cal. Every thought led back to him. I stared out my window, trying to blink back tears and not succeeding. I wiped them away with the back of my hand.

Gradually it dawned on me that I didn't recognize the road we were on. "Where are we going?" I asked. "This isn't the way to my house."

"It's the way to *my* house. I thought it would be better if you washed up first, got the smell of smoke out of your hair and so forth, before you faced your parents."

I nodded, relieved that once again he'd thought it out. My parents—my adoptive parents, really—weren't comfortable with my powers or with me practicing witchcraft. Besides the fact that they're Catholic, they were frightened by what had happened to my birth mother, Maeve Riordan. Sixteen years ago Maeve and my biological father, Angus Bramson, had burned to death. No one knew exactly how it had happened, but it seemed pretty clear that the fact that they were witches had had everything to do with it.

I pressed my hand against my mouth, trying desperately to make sense of the last few weeks. Just a month ago I'd discovered that I was adopted and that by birth I was a descendent of one of the Seven Great Wiccan Clans—a blood witch. My birth parents had died when I was only a baby. Tonight I had almost shared their fate.

And it had been at Cal's hands. At the hands of the guy with whom I'd hoped to share the rest of my life.

Ahead of us, a fat brown rabbit sat frozen in the middle of the icy road, paralyzed by my car's headlight. Hunter brought the car to a stop, and we waited.

"Can you tell me what happened tonight?" he asked, surprisingly gently.

"No." My hand was still pressed against my mouth, and I had to take it away to explain. "Not right now." My voice cracked with a sob. "It hurts too much."

The rabbit came out of its paralysis and scampered to safety on the other side of the road. Hunter pressed the gas pedal, and Das Boot surged forward again. "Right, then," he said. "Later."

Hunter and Sky's house was on a quiet street somewhere near the edge of Widow's Vale. I didn't really pay attention to the route. Now that the adrenaline of escaping the fire was leaking away, I felt exhausted, groggy.

The car pulled to a stop. We were in a driveway beneath a canopy of trees. We got out to the night's chill and walked up a narrow path. I followed Hunter into a living room where a fire burned in a small fireplace. A worn sofa covered in dark blue velvet stood against one wall. One of its legs had broken off, and it listed at a drunken angle. There were two mismatched armchairs across from it, and a wide plank balanced on two wooden crates served as a coffee table.

"You'll need a shower and clean clothes," Hunter told me.

I glanced at a small clock on the mantel. It was nearly nine. I was more than late for dinner. "I've got to call my folks first," I said. "They've probably called the police by now."

Hunter handed me a cordless phone. "Should I tell them about the fire?" I asked him, feeling lost.

He hesitated. "The choice is yours, of course," he said at

last. "But if you do, you'll have a lot of explaining to do."

I nodded. He was right. One more thing I couldn't share with my family.

Nervously I dialed my home number.

My dad answered, and I heard the relief in his voice as I greeted him. "Morgan, where on earth are you?" he asked. "We were about to call the state troopers!"

"I'm at a friend's house," I said, trying to be as honest as I could.

"Are you all right? You sound hoarse."

"I'm okay. But Cal and I . . . we had a fight." I fought to keep my voice steady. "I'm—I'm kind of upset. That's why I didn't call earlier. I'm sorry," I added lamely.

"Well, we were very worried," my dad said. "But I'm glad you're all right. Are you coming home now?"

The front door opened, and Sky walked in. She glanced at me, then looked at Hunter and shook her head. "Not a trace," she said in a low voice.

Ice trickled down my spine. "In a little while, Dad," I said into the phone. "I'll be home in a little while."

Dad sighed. "Don't forget that tomorrow is a school day."

I said good-bye and hung up. "You didn't find them?" I asked Sky anxiously.

"They're gone. They hid their tracks with so many concealing spells that I can't even tell which direction they went," Sky said. "But they're definitely nowhere nearby."

I stood there, feeling my heart beat, not knowing how to process that information. After a moment, Sky took my arm and gently led me upstairs. I was too out of it to notice much more than that there were two doors up there that were closed. The third, in between them, opened into a narrow bathroom.

Sky disappeared through one of the doorways, then reappeared a moment later holding a bathrobe. "You can wear this when you come out," she said. "Leave your clothes outside the door, and I'll throw them in the washer."

I took the robe and closed the door, feeling suddenly self-conscious. I turned and dared a look in the mirror. My nose was red and swollen, my eyes puffy, and my long dark hair matted and flecked with ash. Soot streaked my face and clothes.

I'm hideous, I thought, as Cal's face rose in my mind again. He'd been so incredibly beautiful. How could I ever have believed he could really love someone like me? How could I have been so blind? I was such an idiot.

Clenching my jaw, I stripped down. I opened the door a crack and dropped my clothes in a heap on the hall floor. Then I got into the shower and scrubbed my body and my hair hard, as if the water could wash away more than dirt and smoke, as if it could take my sorrow and terror and rage and sluice them down the drain.

Afterward I dried off and put on the robe. Sky was taller than I was, and the robe bunched at my feet, looking shapeless and drab. I pulled a comb through my wet hair and went back downstairs.

Sky was sitting in one of the armchairs, but as I came down, she rose gracefully to her feet and went up to her room. As she passed me, she let her hand rest briefly on my shoulder.

Hunter stood at the fireplace, feeding a log to the fire. A

small ceramic teapot and two mugs sat on the coffee table. He turned to face me, and I was keenly aware of how good-looking he was.

I settled myself on the sofa, and Hunter sat in a worn armchair. "Better?" he asked.

"A little." My chest and throat weren't quite as sore, and my eyes had stopped stinging.

Hunter's green eyes were locked on me. "I need you to tell me what happened."

I took a deep breath; then I told him how Sky and I had scryed together. How she'd helped me to spy on Cal and his mother in their spell-guarded house as they talked to their coconspirators about killing me if I refused to join them. How I saw that Cal had been assigned to seduce me, to get me onto their side so that my power could be joined with theirs. How I'd learned that they were also after my birth mother's coven tools, objects of enormous power that they wanted to add to their arsenal of magickal weapons. How I'd gone to talk to Cal, how he'd overpowered me with magick and taken me back to his house.

"He put me in a seòmar in the back of the pool house," I said, a vivid picture of the horrible little secret room rising in my mind. "The walls were covered with dark runes. He must have knocked me unconscious. When I came to, I heard Selene arguing with him outside. She was telling him not to do it, not to set it on fire. But Cal said"—my voice broke again—"he said he was solving the problem. He meant me. I was the p-p-problem."

"Shhh," Hunter said softly. Reaching out, he laid his palm flat against my forehead. I felt a tingling warmth spread outward from the spot, like a thousand little bubbles. His eyes held mine as the sensation washed over me, dulling the edge of my pain to the point where I could just bear it.

"Thanks," I said, awed.

He smiled briefly, his face transforming for a moment. Then he said, "Morgan, I'm sorry to press you, but this is important. Did they get your birth mother's tools?"

Maeve had fled her native Ireland after her coven, Belwicket, had been decimated. I had recently found her tools, the ancient tools of her coven. Selene had wanted them badly. "No," I told Hunter. "They're safe. I'd know if they weren't—they're bound to me. Anyway, I hid them."

Hunter poured us each a cup of tea. "Where?"

"Um—under Bree's house. I put them there right before I went to see Cal," I said. It sounded so lame as I said it that I cringed, waiting for Hunter to yell at me.

But he just nodded. "All right. I suppose they'll be safe enough for now, since Cal and Selene have fled. But get them back as soon as you can."

"What can they do with them?" I asked. "Why are they so dangerous?"

"I'm not sure exactly what they could do," Hunter said. "But Selene is very powerful and very skilled in magick, as you know. And some of the tools, the athame and the wand in particular, were made long ago, back before Belwicket renounced the blackness. They've since been purified, of course, but they were made to channel and focus dark energies. I'm sure Selene could find a way to return them to their original state. I imagine, for example, that Maeve's wand in

Selene's hands could be used to magnify the power of the dark wave."

The dark wave. I felt a coldness in the pit of my stomach. The dark wave was the thing that had wiped out Maeve's coven. It had also destroyed Hunter's parents' coven and had forced his mother and father into hiding ten years ago. They were still missing.

No one seemed to know exactly what the dark wave was—whether it was an entity with a will of its own or a force of mindless destruction, like a tornado. All we did know was that where it passed, it left death and horror behind it, entire towns turned to ash. Hunter believed that Selene was somehow connected to the dark wave. But he didn't know how.

I put my head in my hands. "Is all of this happening because Cal and Selene are Woodbane?" I asked in a small voice. Woodbane was the family name of one of the Seven Great Clans of Wicca. To be Woodbane meant, traditionally, to be without a moral compass. Woodbanes throughout history had used any means at their disposal, including calling on dark spirits or dark energy, to become more powerful. Supposedly this had all changed when the International Council of Witches had come into being and made laws to govern the use of magick. But as I was learning, the world of Wicca was as fractured and divided as the everyday world I'd known for the first sixteen years of my life. And there were many Woodbanes who didn't live by the council's laws.

I happened to be Woodbane, too. I hadn't wanted to believe it when I first found out, but the small, red, dagger-shaped birthmark on the inside of my arm was proof of it.

Many, if not most, Woodbanes had one somewhere. It was known as the Woodbane athame, because it looked like the ceremonial dagger that was part of any witch's set of tools.

Hunter sighed, and I was reminded that he was half Woodbane himself. "That's the question, isn't it? I don't honestly know what it means to be Woodbane. I don't know what's nature and what's nurture."

He set down his mug and rose. "I'll see if your clothes are dry. Then I'll run you home."

Sky followed us to my house in her car so that she could drive Hunter home. He and I didn't talk on the way. Whatever calming effect his touch had had on me was entirely gone now, and my mind kept replaying Cal lying to me, shouting at me, using his magick to nearly kill me. How could something that had been so sweet, that felt so good, have turned into this? How could I have been so blind? And why, even now, was some shameful part of me wanting to call to him? Cal, don't leave me. Cal, come back. Oh, God. I swallowed as bile rushed up into my throat.

"Morgan," Hunter said as he pulled up in front of my house. "You do understand, don't you, that you can't let your guard down? Cal may be gone, but it's likely he'll come back."

Come back? Hope, fear, rage, confusion swept over me. "Oh, God." I doubled over in my seat, hugging myself. "Oh, God. I loved him. I feel so *stupid*."

"Don't," Hunter said quietly. I looked up. His face was turned away from me. I saw the plane of his cheek, pale and smooth in the milky starlight that filtered in through Das Boot's windshield.

"I know how much you loved Cal," Hunter said. "And I understand why. There's a lot in him that's truly beautiful. And—and I believe that he loved you, too, in his own way. You didn't imagine that. Even though I was one of the ones telling you otherwise."

He turned to face me then, and we stared at each other. "Look. I know you feel like you'll never get past this. But you will. It won't ever go away, but it *will* stop hurting quite so much. Trust me. I know what I'm talking about."

I was reminded of the time he and I had joined our minds, and I'd seen that he had lost not only his parents but also his brother to dark magick. He'd suffered so much that I felt I could believe him.

He made a movement as if he were going to touch my face with his hand. But he seemed to stop himself and pulled his hand back. "You'd better go in before your parents come out here," he said.

I bit the inside of my cheek so I wouldn't start crying all over again. "Okay," I whispered. I sniffed and looked at my house. The lights were on in the living room.

I felt suddenly awkward. After that moment of connection, should I shake Hunter's hand? Kiss his cheek? In the end I just said, "Thanks for everything."

We both got out of the car. Hunter gave me my keys and headed down the dark street to where Sky waited in her car. I walked up the drive, my body on autopilot. I hesitated at the door. How was I going to act normal around my parents when I felt like I'd been ripped apart?

I opened the front door. The living room was empty, and the house smelled of chocolate chip cookies and wood smoke. There were still embers in the fireplace, and I could smell a faint tinge of the lemon oil that my mom used on the furniture. I heard my parents' voices in the kitchen and the sound of the dishwasher being unloaded.

"Mom? Dad?" I called nervously.

My parents, Sean and Mary Grace Rowlands, came into the living room. "Morgan, you look like you've been crying," my mom said when she caught sight of me. "Was the fight with Cal very bad?"

"I—I broke up with Cal." It wasn't exactly true, but it wasn't the falsehood that shocked me as much as the truth of my situation. Cal and I were no longer together. We were not a couple. We were not going to love each other forever. We were not going to be together again. Ever.

"Oh, honey," said my mom. The sympathy in her voice made me want to cry for the hundredth time that awful night.

"That's too bad," my dad chimed in.

"Um, I also had a little accident in Das Boot," I said. The lie slipped out before I'd even fully formulated it. I just knew I had to explain the crumpled hood of my car somehow.

"An accident?" my dad exclaimed. "What happened? Are you all right? Was anyone else hurt?"

"No one got hurt. I was pulling out of Cal's driveway and I hit a light pole. I kind of messed up the hood of my car." I swallowed. "I guess I was pretty upset."

"Oh my God," Mom said. "That sounds serious! Are you sure you're all right? Maybe we should run you over to the ER and have them take a look at you."

"Mom, I didn't hit my head or anything." I smothered a cough.

"But—" my dad began.

"I'm fine." I cut him off. I had to get to my room before I had a nervous breakdown right in front of them. "I'm just beat, that's all. I really just want to go to bed."

Then, before they could ask any more questions, I fled up the stairs. I was relieved to see that the door to my sister's room was closed. I couldn't handle another explanation. Or even another syllable.

In my room I paused briefly to pet Dagda, my little gray kitten, who was curled up on my desk chair. He mewed a sleepy hello. I went over to my dresser to get out my softest flannel pajamas. But I paused, staring at a tiny gift box on top of my dresser. It was one of the birthday gifts Cal had given me last week: a pair of earrings, golden tigereyes set in silver. I couldn't stop myself from opening the box to look at them again. They were as beautiful as I remembered: the silver swirling in delicate Celtic knots and the stones that were the same color as Cal's eyes. I could still see him, his dark, raggedly shorn hair, his sensual mouth, the golden eyes that seemed to see right into me. The way he used to laugh. The way he had felt like a soul mate from the start.

I laid the earrings on my palm. They gave off a little pool of heat. They're spelled, I realized with a rush of nausea. Goddess, they're just another tool to control me, to spy on me. I remembered thinking, when he gave them to me, that these gifts were wrapped in his love. But the fact was, they were wrapped in his magick.

I couldn't keep them anywhere near me, I realized. I would have to find a safe way to dispose of everything Cal had given me. But not tonight. I stashed the earrings in the back of my closet, together with his other gifts. Then I put on my pajamas.

As I was pulling back my covers, there was a soft knock at my door. A moment later my mom stepped in. "Are you going to be all right?" she asked. Her voice was quiet.

And then the tears were flooding down my cheeks, my defenses completely overwhelmed. I sobbed so hard, my whole body shook.

I felt my mom beside me, her arms encircling me, and I clung to her as I hadn't in years. "My darling," she said into my hair. "My daughter. I'm so sorry. I know how much you must be hurting. Do you want to talk about it?"

I raised my head and met her eyes. "I can't . . . ," I whispered, gasping. "I can't. . . ."

She nodded. "All right," she said. "When you're ready."

When I'd crawled into bed, she pulled the comforter up to my chin and kissed my forehead as if I were six. Reaching over, she turned off my light. "I'm here," she murmured, taking my hand in hers. "It'll be all right."

And so, clutching her hand tightly, I fell asleep.

2.
Changes

I went back to Selene's house tonight after I drove Morgan home. I waited until the police and firefighters were all gone, and then I spent an hour trying to get in, but I couldn't break through the thicket of spells she put round the place. It's bloody frustrating. I felt like chucking a rock through one of those big plate glass windows.

I wonder if Morgan could do it? I know she got into Selene's hidden library without even trying. She is incredibly strong, though incredibly untutored, too.

No. I can't ask her. Not after what she went through at that place. Goddess, the pain in her face tonight—and all over that bastard Cal. It made me sick to see it.

—Giomanach

I drifted awake on Monday, aware that the house was awfully quiet. Was I actually up before my parents or my sister?

It didn't seem possible. They were all morning people, insanely perky long before noon, a trait I could not fathom. It should have been the great tip-off that I was adopted.

I squinted at my clock. Nine forty-eight?

I bolted upright. "Mary K.!" I yelled.

No answer from my sister's room. I cast my senses out and realized I was alone in the house. What is going on? I wondered, sitting up.

A cough tore at my throat. Within the next instant everything that had happened last night came back to me. The enormity of it overwhelmed me. I dropped back against my pillows again and took a deep breath.

Nine forty-eight. Calculus would be starting soon. It suddenly hit me that I would never share my calculus and physics classes with Cal again, and anguish clawed at me. How stupid are you? I asked myself in disgust.

I staggered to my feet and padded downstairs. A note from my mom lay on the kitchen counter.

> Sweetie,
>   I think you need to rest today. Dad gave Mary K. a ride to school, and she'll go to Jaycee's later. There's left-over chili in the fridge for lunch. Give me a call and let me know how you're feeling.
>   Love, Mom
> P.S. I know you won't believe me yet, but I promise you will get over this.

I blinked, feeling both grateful and guilty. There was so much they didn't know; so much I could never tell them.

I stuck a Pop-Tart in the toaster and got a Diet Coke from the fridge. The first sip, though, convinced me it was a mistake. The bubbles of carbonation stung like little pin-pricks as they went down my throat. I made some tea instead and skimmed through the newspapers. The local paper only came out twice a month, and of course there was nothing in *The New York Times* or the *Albany Times Union* about a minor fire in Widow's Vale, two hours away from either city. I could watch the local news later on TV. I won dered if my school would have some kind of explanation for Cal's disappearance.

By the time I'd finished breakfast, it was after ten. For a moment I debated crawling back under the covers with Dagda. But I needed to deal with Cal's gifts right away, so a trip to Practical Magick was in order. I figured the people who ran the shop, Alyce and David, would know what to do.

Then a horrible thought occurred to me: David and Alyce were part of Starlocket, Selene's coven. Could they have had anything to do with what happened to me?

I sank back into the chair, resting my elbows on the kitchen table, my forehead in my hands. My stomach roiled. Had everyone I'd trusted betrayed me? Practical Magick was almost a sanctuary to me; Alyce, in particular, a kind of guide. Even David, who had initially made me feel uncomfortable, was turning out to be someone whose friendship I valued.

Think, I told myself. I'd felt awkward with David but never threatened. I hadn't heard their voices while I was trapped in the pool house. And Hunter had explained to me that Selene created covens wherever she went—and then destroyed the non-Woodbane members. Neither David nor

Alyce was Woodbane. They would have been in danger from Selene as well—wouldn't they?

It's okay, I told myself. David and Alyce are my friends.

I called my mom at her office and thanked her for letting me stay home.

"Well, I know that you share some classes with Cal," Mom said. "I thought it might be hard to see him today."

Her words reminded me: she didn't even know he was gone. My stomach knotted up again. My mom thought all I was suffering from was my very first broken heart. That was certainly true, but it was also so much more than that, Cal's betrayal so much deeper.

"I'm sorry, sweetie, but I've got to run," she said. "I've got an appointment to show a house in Taunton. Will you be all right? Want me to come home at lunch?"

"No, I'm okay," I said. "I think I'll go out and run some errands."

"Staying busy is a good idea," she said. "And if you feel like calling later, just to talk, I'll be here most of the afternoon."

"Thanks." I hung up and went upstairs. I changed into jeans and a heavy ski sweater that my Aunt Maureen had given me last Christmas. I don't ski, and the sweater was kind of snowflaky for my taste, but I was cold, and it was the warmest thing I owned.

I went into my closet, where I had shoved Cal's gifts. My hands shook as I put them in my backpack. I set my jaw and willed myself not to grieve over them, over him. Then I grabbed my parka and hurried out of the house.

I drove north in my battered, rattly car, beneath bleak,

wintry skies that seemed leached of all color. Despite the salt on the roads, a thin sheet of ice covered the ground. All the cars were moving slowly. I switched on the radio, hoping for the local news, but instead got a weather report stating that the temperature was currently eighteen degrees and would drop to ten by evening. With the wind chill, it was even more brutal.

I pulled into a parking spot right in front of Practical Magick; for a change, parking was easy, as the block was practically empty. Only after I had climbed out of my car did I remember that there was one more gift from Cal, the one I'd loved best of all: the pentacle that he had worn around his neck. It was somewhere on the floor of my car, where I'd let it fall the day before when it had hit me that Cal was using it to enhance his control over me. I leaned down, searched the damp floor mats, and found the little silver circle with its five-pointed star. Without looking at it, I slipped it into the outer pocket of my pack.

I pushed through the heavy glass doors into Practical Magick. The shop was dark and cozy; half of it given to books on every aspect of Wicca, the occult, and New Age spiritual practices; the other half filled with a huge variety of supplies: candles, herbs, powders, crystals, ritual tools like athames, pentacles, robes, even cauldrons. The warm air was scented with herbs and incense. It all felt familiar, reassuring, safe—all feelings I had in very short supply at the moment.

I was surprised to see a customer in the shop, since there weren't any cars out front. Alyce was talking to a young woman who wore a sling with a baby in it and was holding the hand of a boy who looked to be about four years old.

As the woman spoke to her, Alyce nodded, dislodging several strands of gray hair from her long braid. She tucked them back in without ever taking her blue eyes from the young woman's face. It looked like a serious conversation. I wandered along the rows of books, waiting until they were done. I wanted to be able to talk to Alyce and David privately.

Then I heard more voices and saw an elderly couple emerge from behind the curtain that blocked off the tiny back room that David used as an office. They looked upset, as the woman talking with Alyce did. I wondered what was going on. Were there all kinds of magickal emergencies requiring Alyce and David's help today?

The elderly couple spoke with Alyce and the young woman. From the way they were behaving, they all seemed to know one another. They must be the people who lived upstairs, I realized. Practical Magick was on the ground floor of a three-story building. There were apartments above it, but I had never seen any of the tenants before. That would explain why there were no cars outside and why the elderly couple wore only sweaters.

They all left together. Alyce watched them for a moment, shook her head sadly, and then went back behind the counter.

I studied her quietly. Could she have had any part in what had happened to me?

Sensing my gaze, Alyce glanced up. "Morgan," she said, and I could see nothing but concern in her face. She came out from around the counter and took both my hands. "Hunter came by this morning and told us what happened. Are you all right?"

I nodded, looking at her. I let my senses seek for danger from her. I sensed nothing.

"Let's go in the back and talk," Alyce said. "I'll put the teakettle on."

I followed her behind the counter to the small back room, where David, the other clerk, sat at the square, battered table he used as a desk. An open ledger, its columns filled with numbers, lay in front of him. David, who was in his early thirties, was prematurely gray, a trait that he said was typical of his clan, the Burnhides. Today his face looked drawn and weary, as if he were aging to match his hair.

"Morgan, " he said, "I was horrified to hear what happened to you. Please, sit down."

He closed the ledger as Alyce put a mixture of dried herbs into a metal tea ball. Then she turned to face me. "We owe you an apology," she said. David nodded his agreement.

I waited nervously. An apology for what?

"We were too slow to see what Selene was really after," David said. "Too slow to stop her."

I could feel truth, and sorrow, in his statement. My nerves began to unwind.

"It wasn't your fault," I said. It felt strange to have these adult witches apologizing to me. "I should have seen through Selene and . . . and the rest of them." I couldn't bring myself to say Cal's name.

The kettle on the hot plate began to steam, and Alyce poured the boiling water into a teapot. She set it on a trivet to let the tea steep.

"Selene is a very seductive woman," David said. "All of Starlocket was taken in by her, even those of us who should have been wary. Cal might have been the only one who truly knew her nature."

"She's pure evil," I said angrily. The force of my words surprised me.

David raised one silver eyebrow. "It's more complex than that, I think. Very few things are purely black or white."

"Plotting to kidnap or kill me?" I demanded. "To steal my mother's coven's tools? Doesn't that count as evil?"

"Yes, of course," David said. He wasn't flustered by my outburst. In fact, it occurred to me that I'd never seen him flustered about anything. "Her actions were evil. But her intentions may have been more complicated than that."

"Her intentions aren't at issue," Alyce said, and I heard a note of steel in her voice.

David looked thoughtful but didn't say anything.

Alyce poured the tea. "Mint, motherwort, lemongrass, and a pinch of catnip. It's a very soothing brew," she announced, as if she wanted to change the subject. She sat down and took my hand. "This must be so awful for you," she said.

All I could do was nod. I took a deep breath. "Did you know they were both Woodbane?" I blurted. I hadn't realized how much that troubled me until this moment.

Alyce and David exchanged glances. "Yes," said David. "But that name doesn't mean what it used to."

"Morgan," Alyce said, closing her hand over mine, "you know that being Woodbane doesn't make you evil. A person chooses his or her own way."

"I guess," I mumbled. In a way I wanted to believe that Cal had had no choice but to be evil because of his Woodbane blood. But that would mean that I didn't either. I sighed. Wicca had seemed such a beautiful thing at first. How had it all become so complicated and frightening?

"If you need anything," David said, "If you have a question, need someone to talk to . . ."

"A shoulder to cry on," Alyce added. "Please, come to us. We are so sorry we weren't able to protect you from Selene. You are so new to this world, so vulnerable."

"Maybe you can help me now," I said, pulling my pack up into my lap. I removed the things I'd packed. "I got some birthday gifts from . . . from Cal." There, I'd said it. "Plus his pentacle. They're all spelled. What should I do with them?"

"Burn them," David advised. "Cast a purification spell so that even the ashes will be free of his magick."

"I agree," said Alyce. "You have to break their powers. They could still be acting on you, influencing you, as long as they exist."

"Okay." As I gazed at the pile of gifts, the enormity of Cal's betrayal rose up and threatened to drown me again. I swallowed, fighting back a sob as I put them back into my pack.

"It will be hard, but it's something only you can do for yourself," Alyce said. "If you'd like, you can come back here after the ritual."

"Maybe I will," I said. I took another sip of tea.

The bells over the front door jangled, indicating that someone had come into the store. "I'd better go and see who that is," Alyce said, standing up.

The phone rang, and David looked at it, frowning. "Here we go again. Would you two excuse me, please?"

A shadow seemed to pass over Alyce's face. "Come on,

Morgan," she said. "Let me take care of this customer. Then I'll help you find a purification spell. A really strong one."

In the main room I skimmed the bookcases, looking for purification spells, while I waited for Alyce.

Suddenly I heard David's voice raised from the back room. It was so unusual to hear him excited that I glanced up, startled. "Look, it's not just me. Two families will lose their homes!" he shouted. "I need more time." Then he said something else, but his voice had dropped to its normal, quiet pitch, which put an end to my eavesdropping.

I glanced at Alyce. Her face wore its usual air of calm, but I saw that her shoulders had tightened. They only relaxed once David's voice returned to normal.

After her customer paid for his purchase, she joined me. She scanned the shelves, then took down a slender book titled *Rituals for Purification and Protection*. "Try page forty-three. I think you'll find what you need for dealing with Cal's gifts."

As I read through the spell, David's voice rose again, and of course I listened. I couldn't help it. "I can't afford that, and you know it!" he shouted.

Alyce gave me a quick glance. She knew I had heard David, so I figured, why not just ask? "Alyce, what's going on?" I asked bluntly. "Who is David talking to?"

Alyce took a deep breath. "It sounds like he's talking to Stuart Afton or, more likely, Afton's lawyers."

"But why?" I asked. "Is something wrong? And who's Stuart Afton?"

"It's a long story," Alyce said. "David's Aunt Rosaline, who owned the store—this entire building, actually—died last week."

"I'm sorry to hear that." So much for my witch senses. I

hadn't even detected David's grief. My own problems had overwhelmed me. "Is he okay?"

Alyce bit her lip as if she was trying to decide how much to say. "Well, Rosaline's death wasn't unexpected. She'd been ill for a while. But that's only the beginning, I'm afraid. David had always assumed that, as her only living relative, he'd inherit the shop. But Rosaline died without a will and, unbeknownst to David, heavily in debt to a local real estate developer named Stuart Afton."

Now I realized why the name had sounded familiar. "Afton as in Afton Enterprises?" I'd seen the sign on a gravel pit just down the road from Unser's Auto Repair, where I always took Das Boot for service.

Alyce nodded. "Rosaline had been borrowing for years to keep the store afloat, using the building itself as collateral. The store barely makes any money, and Rosaline couldn't bear to raise the rent on the Winstons and the Romerios."

"Who are the Winstons and the Romerios?" I asked.

"They were all here when you arrived, actually," Alyce replied. "Lisa Winston is the woman I was talking to; she lives with her two boys on the top floor. The Romerios were that sweet old couple that came out of David's office. They were living on the second floor when Rosaline bought the building, years ago—that's how far back they go. They never had any children; they live on social security." She shook her head. "It would be impossible for them to move. And it would be a struggle for Lisa Winston. Her husband left her with those two little boys and nothing else."

I shook my head, confused. "But what's the problem? Why would they have to move?"

"Well, Rosaline didn't borrow from a bank; she borrowed from Afton. I'm not sure why—maybe the bank wouldn't give her a loan. Anyway, Afton essentially took over her mortgage. He doesn't have to follow the same rules as a bank. And now he wants the loan repaid in full at once, or the building is his." Alyce sighed. "Unless David can raise the money to repay him or Afton forgives the debt, this building will go to Afton. That was obviously his plan all along. He owns the buildings on either side already. Apparently he's been soliciting buyers, and rumor has it one of the big bookstore chains is interested in buying the whole block of properties and converting it into one big superstore."

"So Afton's just going to throw the tenants out?" I asked.

"More or less," Alyce agreed. "He can't flat out evict them, but he can raise their rents to market value, which comes to the same thing. If they lose those apartments, they'll never find anything else they can afford in this area."

"And Afton doesn't care?"

Alyce shrugged. "He's a businessman. He doesn't like losing money. Believe me, David and I have spent this entire week on the phone, trying everything we could think of to raise the money, but without much success."

My stomach dropped as the implication hit me. "What will happen to the store?"

Alyce looked at me with a steady gaze. "We'll sell off the stock and close. We can't afford rent in this area, either."

I looked at her in dismay. "Oh, no. You can't close. We all need you here, as a resource." Panic made my breath come faster. Having lost the anchor of Cal in my life, the idea of losing Practical Magick, my haven, threatened to push me over the edge.

"I know, my dear. It's a shame. But some things are out of our hands," Alyce said.

"No," I said. "We can't just accept this." I was stunned that she seemed so calm.

"Everything in life has its own cycle," Alyce said gently. "And the cycle always includes a death of sorts. It's the only way you get to a new cycle, to regeneration. If it's time for Practical Magick to come to an end, it will end."

"It's awful," I said in dismay. "I can't believe Afton can do this. Why can't someone get through to him, show him what he's doing?"

"Because he doesn't want to see," Alyce replied. Her brow furrowed. "I'm worried more about David than myself. I can always go back to teaching. But I'm not sure what he'll do. This store has been more or less his home since he got out of college. It will be much harder for him than for me."

I clenched my teeth in frustration, wondering if there was anything at all I could do. Organize a protest? A petition? A sit-in? Surely there must be some spell that could be done? But I wasn't supposed to do spells. That was the one thing all the more experienced witches agreed upon—that I didn't have enough knowledge yet. Besides, I told myself, if there were spells, well, David and Alyce would surely have already done them.

"All right, enough gloom," said Alyce briskly. "Tell me, do you have Maeve's cauldron?" Alyce knew I'd found my birth mother's tools.

"No."

"Well, pick out a nice cauldron, then," she said.

"Do I need one?" I asked.

"It's something every witch should have as part of her tools," she explained. "And you need it to make the fire to burn Cal's gifts. You want the fire contained in something round that you can circle with protection spells."

I went and chose a small cauldron from the ones on display and brought it back to the counter. Alyce nodded her approval. "Do you have all the herbs you need?" she asked.

I checked my spell, and Alyce filled a small paper bag with the ingredients I needed. "Make sure that before you start, you purify the cauldron with salt water," she said. "And then purify it again when you're done to ensure that none of Cal's magick lingers."

"I will," I promised. "Thanks, Alyce. And please tell David how sorry I am about his aunt and the store. If there's anything I can do to help . . ."

"Don't worry about us," she replied. "This is a time to heal yourself, Morgan."

After I'd paid and left Practical Magick, depression settled on me again. Cal had been not only my first love, but my first teacher as well. I hadn't realized this before, but right up until the moment Alyce told me the store might close, some part of me had already assumed that even without Cal, I'd have a place to learn about Wicca. Now it looked like I was going to lose that, too.

3.
Purified

December, 1982

A year ago I had no children. Now I have two—and I can't be a father to either of them.

Cal, the elder, was born in June. I love him; how could I help it? He's so beautiful, so sweet and trusting. But I can't bear it when he looks at me with his mother's golden eyes. I can't bear the growing fear that he is Selene's creation, that she'll mold him to follow her in her madness and that nothing I do can stop it.

Yet still, I feel bound to stay. Bound to try to save him.

Giomanach, my younger son, was born just three nights ago. I felt, across an ocean and a continent, Fiona's pain and joy as he came out of her body. I ache to be with her, with my dearest love, my soul mate—and I ache to see my newborn son. But I don't dare go to them for fear that Selene will take some terrible vengeance on them.

Goddess. I'm being ripped in two. How much longer can I bear this?

—Maghach

I made one quick detour on the way home, pulling into Bree's driveway. I climbed out and glanced around to see if anyone was watching me. Even though it was noon on Monday in a residential neighborhood and not many people were around, I whispered, "You see me not: I am but a shadow," as I hurried around to the side of Bree's house.

I knelt next to a big, winter-bare lilac that grew outside the dining-room window and reached deep into the crawl space hidden by the cluster of woody stems. Tucked behind a piling was a rusted metal box. I'd hidden it there less than twenty-four hours earlier, on my way to see Cal.

I pulled the box out carefully. It contained my most precious possessions—the tools that Cal, Selene, and the people with them had almost killed me for. Tucking the box and its contents under my coat, I hurried back to my car.

When I got home, I glanced at the kitchen clock. I had a few hours before anyone got home. It was time to get rid of Cal's gifts.

I read over the spell Alyce had recommended. As she'd advised, I purified the cauldron first with boiling, salted water, then with plain salt rubbed over the interior and exterior. In my room I opened the metal box and looked through Maeve's tools. I took out the athame. Since I was planning to perform the ritual in our yard, I decided against using Maeve's green silk robe. You never know when a meter reader will show up or a neighbor will traipse into the yard, chasing after a dog. It wasn't a good idea to risk being seen in full witch regalia.

I was about to close the box when my fingertips brushed against my mother's wand. It was made of black wood, inlaid with thin lines of silver and gold. Four small rubies studded its tip. I'd never used it before, but now I closed one hand around it and instinctively knew it would focus my energy, concentrate and store my power.

The ground was covered with a thick, crunchy sheet of snow. The temperature must have been close to the promised ten degrees; it was bitterly cold. The wind was battering sky, trees, and ground as if determined to whip the warmth from the earth.

Carrying the cauldron and the rest of my supplies, I crossed the yard to a big oak in the back. In a book of Celtic lore, I'd read that the oak was considered a guardian. I stared up into its bare branches, realizing that I actually did feel safer beneath it. I knew that the tree would lend its energy and protection to my ritual.

I set down the cauldron and began to collect fallen branches, shaking off the snow. Giving thanks to the oak for its kindling, I broke the branches and arranged them in the cauldron. Then, using Maeve's athame, I traced a circle in the snow. I sprinkled salt over the line traced by the athame, and I started to feel the earth's power moving through me. I drew the symbols for the four directions and for fire, water, earth, and sky, invoking the Goddess with each one.

I brushed the snow off a boulder and sat down, trying to ignore the cold wind. Closing my eyes, I began to follow my breath, aware of the rise and fall of my chest, the rhythm of my heartbeat, the blood coursing through my veins.

Gradually my awareness deepened. I felt the roots of the oak tree stretching through the frozen ground beneath the circle, reaching toward me. I felt the earth itself echoing with all the years that our family had lived in this house. It was as if all the love in my adoptive family had penetrated the earth, become part of it, and was now surging up to steady me.

I was ready. Opening my eyes, I put the herbs that Alyce had given me into the cauldron. Most of them I recognized: a lump of myrrh, its scent unmistakable, dried patchouli leaves, and wood betony. Two of them I didn't recognize, but as I added them, their names came to me: olibanum tears and small pieces of a root called ague. Finally I added a few drops of pine and rue oil and mixed the ingredients until I felt their essences swirl together.

I concentrated on the cauldron. Fire, I thought. A moment later a spark flickered, and I heard the sound of flames crackling. A thin line of smoke rose from the cauldron.

"Goddess, I ask your help," I began. I glanced at the spell book. "These gifts were given to bind me. Take them into your fire, cleanse them of their dark magick, and render them harmless."

Then, swallowing hard, I took Cal's gifts and one by one dropped them into the cauldron. The beautiful batik blouse whose colors reminded me of a storm at sunset, the book of herbal magick, the earrings, the pentacle, even the blood-stone he'd given me at our last circle. The flames crackled, licked at the rim of the cauldron. I watched the pages of the book curl into glowing whorls of ash. The burning ink gave off a faint, acrid smell. Wisps of glowing thread drifted upward as the batik blouse was consumed by the fire.

It burned hotter, hotter, until it gave off an incandescence that was almost too much for my eyes. The flames leapt to meet the wind high above the cauldron. I gasped, my heart aching with sadness. There, in the center of the white-hot flames, I saw Cal exactly as he had been when he gave me my gifts, a look of pure tenderness on his face. I felt myself falling deeper then, my heart opening to him the way a flower opens to the sun. Tears blurred my vision.

"No," I said, suddenly furious that here, in *my circle,* Cal's magick was still rising up to control me. I reached for Maeve's wand and aimed it at the cauldron. I felt my power pour into it and intensify. Beyond that I felt the power of Maeve and her mother, Mackenna, high priestesses both. I began to move deasil, chanting the words from the book aloud:

> *"Earth and air, flame and ice,*
> *Take darkness from me.*
> *Cleanse these things of ill intent.*
> *Let this spell cause no harm nor return any on me."*

On the last words of the spell the flames crackled, as if in answer to me, then died out completely. A white, nearly transparent smoke rose. The wand in my hand felt weightless. I gently laid it on the ground.

After a moment I gathered my courage and peered into the cauldron. The blouse was gone entirely, as was the book. There were a few darkened lumps of metal, which I took to be the earrings and the pentagram. The tigereyes seemed to be gone. I could still see the shape of the bloodstone, though, covered in a fine ash. I touched the edge of the cauldron. It was already cool, despite the white-hot flames that had blazed there just moments earlier.

I reached in for the bloodstone. White ash fell from it; it was cool to the touch. I gingerly extended my senses, examining it for any trace of Cal's magick. I couldn't find any.

My fist tightened around it, and something deep inside me snapped. It was a crackling, heartrending release, as if the ritual had broken not only Cal's magickal bonds on me, but my own bonds on my reined-in pain and anger. I flung the bloodstone away as hard as I could. "You bastard, Cal!" I screamed into the bitter wind. "You bastard!"

Then I dropped to my knees, sobbing. How could he have done this to me? How could he have taken something as precious as love and corrupted it so horribly? I crouched, praying to the Goddess to heal my heart.

It was a long time before I straightened up again. When I did, I felt that magick had left the circle. Things were back to normal—whatever normal was.

I opened the circle, grabbed my tools, and took them back into the house. I returned the tools to their old hiding place in the HVAC vent in the upstairs hallway. I made a mental note to find a new hiding place soon. I repurified the cauldron with salt water before stuffing it in the back of my closet. Then I took a hot shower and finally did what I'd wanted to do since that morning.

I got Dagda, crawled into bed, and went back to sleep.

4.
Celebration

August, 1984

I've made my choice, if you can call it a choice. I'm with Fiona now, back home in England. Our second son will be born in a week, and I simply could not stay away any longer. She is my mùirn beatha dàn, my soul's true mate.

I think—I hope—that Selene has at last accepted this. When I left this time, she didn't plead. She said only, "Remember the threefold law. All that you do comes back to you." She turned away, and I watched Cal carefully copy her. I've lost him. He is wholly Selene's now.

Giomanach is so changed from the last time I saw him. He's nearly two years old now, no longer a baby but a wiry little boy with hair like bleached corn silk and Fiona's dancing green eyes. He's a happy child but still shy and a little fearful around me. I try not to let him see how it hurts me.

I try, too, not to think too often of Cal, and of the battle that I lost.
  —Maghach

"Morgan." My sister was sitting on the edge of the bed, shaking my shoulder. "Mom asked me to wake you up."

I opened my eyes and realized it was dark outside. I felt like I'd been asleep for days. "What time is it?" I asked groggily.

"Five-thirty." Mary K. turned on the light on my night table, and I saw the concern in her warm brown eyes. "Aunt Eileen and Paula are on their way over for dinner. They should be here any minute. Hey, Mom told me about you and Cal. And I saw Das Boot. Are you okay?"

I drew in a shaky breath, then nodded. Something had shifted during the purification ceremony. Though I still felt deeply wounded, I didn't have quite the same sense of hopelessness I'd had this morning. "I've been better, but I'll live."

"Cal wasn't in school today," Mary K. said. She hesitated. "There's a rumor going around that he and his mom left town over the weekend. That there was some kind of suspicious fire on their property and now they've disappeared."

"They did leave, it's true," I said. I sighed. "Look, I can't talk about this right now. I'll tell you the whole story soon. But you have to promise to keep it to yourself."

"Okay." She looked solemnly at me, then went through the connecting door to her room.

I pulled on a pair of sweats and a red thermal top and brushed my long hair into a ponytail. Then I went downstairs. In the front hall I heard the doorbell, then a babble of excited voices. "What's going on?" I asked as I went out to greet them. They all sounded cheerful and happy.

"We made an offer on a house today, and it was accepted!" Aunt Eileen told me. When my aunt Eileen and her girlfriend, Paula Steen, decided to move in together, my mom had made it her personal mission to find them the house of their dreams.

Moments later we were all gathered around the dining-room table. Mary K. set out silverware and plates, my dad set out wineglasses, and Mom, Aunt Eileen, and Paula opened container after container of takeout food.

I sniffed the air, not recognizing the smells of either Chinese or Indian food, the two usual choices. "Wow. Smells great. What'd you bring?"

"We splurged at Fortunato's," Paula told me. Fortunato's was a trendy gourmet place that had opened a couple of years ago in Widow's Vale. Our family didn't shop there much, due to their insane prices.

"What's your pleasure?" Aunt Eileen asked. "We've got filet mignon with wild mushrooms, herb potatoes, cold salmon, asparagus vinaigrette, spinach salad, clam fritters, and chicken dijonnaise."

"And save room for chocolate-hazelnut cake," Paula added.

"Oh my God, I'm never going to be able to move again," Mary K. moaned.

Paula popped the cork on a champagne bottle and poured it into glasses as we all took our seats. She even gave Mary K. and me about a swallow each, though I noticed my mom raise her eyebrows as Aunt Eileen handed the glasses to us.

"A toast!" Paula said, and lifted her own glass high. "To our new, absolutely perfect home and the absolutely brilliant real estate agent who found it for us!"

My mom laughed. "May you always be happy there!"

We began passing around the food. It felt good to see everyone so cheerful, even Mary K., who had been looking pretty down since she and her boyfriend, Bakker, had broken up. I was glad to be able to focus on someone's good news. I felt myself start to relax, felt my anxiety recede a bit.

"So tell me all about this perfect house," I said to Eileen.

"It's in Taunton," Eileen began, naming a town about ten miles north of us. "It's a little house with bay windows, set back from the street, with a beautiful garden out back. Wood-burning stove downstairs and a fireplace in the master bedroom. The only bad part is, it's covered with ugly green vinyl siding."

"Which is old and needs to be replaced, anyway," Mom stuck in. "Apart from that, it oozes charm."

"Yeah." Paula grinned. "Just ask the realtor."

"When do you think you'll move in?" Mary K. asked Aunt Eileen.

Aunt Eileen had just taken a huge bite of spinach salad, so Mom answered for her. "The closing is scheduled for next week, after the inspection," she said.

"That's fantastic!" Mary K. said. "You could actually be in by next weekend."

Aunt Eileen took Paula's hand and with her other hand crossed her fingers. "That's what we're hoping," she said.

The rest of dinner went by quickly, with talk of moving plans, house plans, and a heated discussion about how many pets they would adopt once they were settled. Paula was a veterinarian, so Aunt Eileen thought they should have a good menagerie, including several cats and dogs and a rabbit or two. By the time we got to dessert, everyone was laughing.

All at once my smile froze into place as I felt Hunter on our front walk outside. His presence always had a weird effect on me. The doorbell rang a moment later, and I stood quickly. "I'll get it," I said.

I went to the front hall and opened the door. Hunter stood there in a thick green sweater that perfectly matched his eyes. His hands were shoved into the pockets of a worn brown leather jacket that emphasized his broad shoulders.

"You weren't in school today," he stated.

"Hello to you, too," I said dryly.

He ducked his head and kicked snow off his boot. "Uh, right. Hello. How are you feeling?"

"Better, thanks."

He brought his gaze back up to mine, his eyes glinting in the reflection from the little light over the door. "As I was saying—you weren't in school."

My forehead crinkled. Had he gone to my school to check up on me? Was Hunter actually concerned about me?

I must have been staring at him because I noticed the tips of his ears begin to turn pink. Was he blushing? Surely not. Not Hunter. He must really be cold.

"Morgan, who is it?" my mom called.

"Um—it's my friend Hunter," I called back. "I'll just be a second."

"Well, invite him in and shut the door. You're letting in cold air."

Silently I held the door, and Hunter stepped inside. "We need to talk," he said.

I knew he was right, but I wasn't ready yet. "It's not a good time."

"I don't mean about Cal," he said. "I mean about Cirrus." Cirrus was the coven that Cal had started. I was a member, along with Robbie, Jenna Ruiz, Sharon Goodfine, Ethan Sharp, and Matt Adler. Bree had originally been part of Cirrus, too, but when she and I split up over Cal, she and Raven Meltzer had formed Kithic, a coven that was now led by Hunter's cousin Sky.

"Cirrus?" I repeated, confused. "What about it?"

"With Cal gone, you need someone else to lead it. An initiated witch."

I hadn't even thought about that. With Cirrus, Cal had opened up the world of Wicca to me, permanently altering my world. His betrayal had left a deep black hole in my life, and my few new support systems were now being sucked away into it.

I didn't want to lose the coven. "I could ask Alyce or David if they'll take over."

"Alyce and David are already part of Starlocket. I hear Alyce has been asked to lead it now that Selene is gone," Hunter said.

I was silent, thinking, and then Hunter broke in.

"I want to lead Cirrus," he said.

Now I was seriously at sea. "Why?" I asked. "You don't know any of us. You don't even live here. Not permanently, anyway."

"I'll probably be here for a while. I've asked the council

to give me time to come up with new leads on Cal and Selene. I want to see if I can track them down."

"But you don't know how long that will take," I argued. "Anyway, there are five other people in our coven. They might have something to say about who leads us."

"I already discussed it with them," Hunter said. "I went to your school today. That's how I know you weren't there."

So he hadn't gone there out of concern for me. To my surprise, I felt a stab of disappointment. Then my anger rose. How could he be so presumptuous? "So you talked to them and they said yes? You're it?"

"We're going to see how it goes," he said cautiously. "There's a circle tomorrow night at my house at seven. I hope you'll be there. I think it would be good for . . . everyone."

"A circle on a Tuesday night?"

"We can't wait until Saturday," Hunter said. "It's important that Cirrus re-form quickly. When a circle is broken in this way, it can be devastating to the members. Besides, we don't know what magick Cal might have used on the members. I've asked everyone to bring the stones Cal gave them so we can purify them. You should bring yours, too, along with anything else he gave you."

"I already purified everything," I said, and felt a childish triumph when I saw the surprise in his eyes. Now maybe he'd stop being so superior, so remote, making me feel like he was ten years older than me rather than two.

Even as the thoughts formed, I knew I wasn't being fair to him. He really was trying to help. But his very competence irked me, made me feel clumsy, naïve.

He must have sensed a change in my attitude and figured the circle issue was a done deal, because he moved on. "Now, the second thing," he said, "is you. You've come into quite a birthright—far more power than most blood witches ever experience, and Belwicket's tools besides. But you know only the most rudimentary things about how to focus and control your power. And you know even less about how to protect yourself."

I took it as an accusation and felt anger flare again. "I've only known I was a blood witch for a month. I know I have a long way to go."

Hunter sighed. "All I'm saying is that you've got a hell of a lot of catching up to do. Most blood witches are initiated at age fourteen, after studying for years. Witches need to know the history of Wicca and the Seven Great Clans; the rituals of the Goddess and the God and the eight great Sabbats; herbalism; the basics of numerology; the proper use of talismans and runes; the properties of minerals, metals, and stones and how they interact with the cycles of the celestial bodies. The full correspondences; reading auras; spells of protection, healing, binding, and banishment. And though it's more advanced, you really ought to learn about the Guardians of the Watchtowers—"

A sudden burst of laughter came from the kitchen, where Aunt Eileen and Paula and my family were lingering over coffee. It sounded so safe and comforting in there, a world I was not fully part of anymore, a world I had taken for granted. An awful thought occurred to me. "Is my family in danger?" I blurted out.

Hunter ran a hand through his pale blond hair. Tiny crystals of ice had beaded up in it, so now bits of it stuck up in spiky tufts, making him look about eight years old.

"I don't think so," he said. "At least, not now. With Selene's plan exposed, I suspect she and her cronies will lie low for a while. You have a window of safety here, which is why it's vital that you don't waste it. You need to begin studying."

I gnawed my thumbnail. He was right.

"I have some books that I bought at Practical Magick," I told him. "I haven't read them cover to cover, but I've skimmed them." I told him the titles. "And of course I've read most of Maeve's Book of Shadows."

He nodded approvingly. "Those are all good. Keep working with them and we'll talk in a few days. Write down any questions you have. I'll give you a reading list after I have a better sense of what you know."

"Hey." Mary K. came out into the hall. "Hunter, right? How are you?"

"Fine, thanks," he said, flashing her a surprisingly warm smile. "You?"

"Good." Mary K. twisted a strand of auburn hair around her finger.

Was she *flirting* with him? "Hunter's got to go now," I said.

He looked at me, then nodded. "Good night," he called to my sister. To me he said, "You look tired. Get some sleep."

"What a hottie," Mary K. said as the door clicked shut behind him.

"Oh, please," I groaned, then went back to the kitchen to join the group.

5.
Darkness

With Athar's help, I broke the warding spells today. It took the two of us the better part of the day—Athar was annoyed because I made her take a day off from her job.

But I found nothing useful inside. If Selene did leave anything, it's locked in that library of hers, and I can't get at it. The council is sending a fellow down from Boston next week to help me bind the house in spells. Perhaps he'll be able to help me get in. I will not ask Morgan for her help. It's clear that she dislikes me enough already.

I wish she didn't. There's something in her eyes, in the way she holds her head, that somehow draws me to her.

—Giomanach

Something was after me, I could feel it. Deep darkness was surrounding me, trying to find me, to envelop me. I tried to make the rune signs for protection, but I couldn't lift my hands: my fingers weren't working. I'd been bound, just as Cal had bound me to entrap me.

Smoke and flames burned in the back of my throat, and I heard a voice screaming, "Not again!" Somehow I knew the voice belonged to my birth mother, Maeve.

Then faces rose up out of the smothering darkness: Selene and Cal. I begged them to leave me alone. I pushed my lips together tightly, knowing, somehow, that they wanted me to breathe in the darkness, wanted it to become a part of me.

Just as I felt myself about to suffocate, I saw a tiny sliver of light. The faces of Cal and Selene dissolved as the light approached. And then I began to see a new face in its midst.

Hunter.

I woke up, sweaty and gasping for breath. My heart raced, pounding hard in my chest. I pushed my hair away from my damp forehead and looked around the room. I was in my own bedroom. I was alone. Dagda was sleeping on a pillow that had fallen to the floor. It was still pitch dark outside my window.

I shuddered. The dream had been so intense, it felt like it was still with me. I pulled at the sheets. They were completely wrapped around my body. I let out a shaky laugh. No wonder I'd thought I was being smothered. Those sheets were wound as tightly as a straitjacket. I struggled free, then reached over to my bedside table and flicked on the lamp. Not so good. The lamp cast spooky shadows all around my room. I got up and turned on my overhead light. Dagda stretched and blinked sleepily. I picked him up and brought him back into bed with me.

"It was just a nightmare," I told my purring kitten. "It's just my brain trying to process all that I've been through."

I pulled the comforter up around my shoulders. I'd gone from sweaty to freezing. Was my window open? I glanced over, but no, it was shut. I still felt anxious, unsettled. My heart started its syncopated beat again. Was it just the aftermath of the dream, or was I picking up something with my witch senses?

Cradling Dagda close to my body, I got up and went to the window. I took in deep breaths, trying to calm my mind. Dagda squirmed, so I put him down. I didn't want to be distracted.

Willing myself to breathe evenly, I opened myself to the night. I could feel the sting of frosty air on my face as my senses moved out of my cozy bedroom and into the backyard. The world was quiet under its blanket of snow, and the trees themselves seemed to be asleep. The houses were filled with sleeping bodies; a car drove slowly along the road. Beyond that, I didn't get much sensation, just vague cold.

Then a wave of nausea hit me. My veins felt like they were filled with cold sludge. The only other time I'd felt anything like this horrible sensation was when Cal had used magick to bind me.

There was dark magick in Widow's Vale tonight. I knew that with certainty.

Stay clear, stay calm, a voice said in my head. Was it my own? Don't fight the sensation, the voice told me. Examine it.

As I stopped fighting the nausea, it seemed to dissipate. I realized that I wasn't being acted upon. This wasn't an attack—it felt oddly impersonal. The energy, whatever it was, wasn't directed at me. It was as if I'd gotten a whiff of something really foul but hadn't actually come into contact with it.

But what was it? And where was it coming from?

Suddenly I could see the field where Cal had brought us for our very first circle. I couldn't make out what was happening there, but I was certain that I was seeing the place where the magick was being worked.

I gasped. It could only mean one thing. Cal and Selene were back. Who else would go to that particular field? They were there, working their dark spells. Whatever they were doing right now wasn't aimed at me. But it was only a matter of time before they came for me.

6.
A New Circle

Kennet Muir, my council mentor, rang from London to say he'd got a new assignment for me. There was a cat found in a suburb of Montreal with its throat cut, and the council fears a rogue coven may have resurrected the blood rituals that were banned in the nineteenth century.

On the strength of one dead cat! It's ridiculous: it's a fool's errand, and I told Kennet so. I told him I needed to stay here, that I had many things to finish. He finally agreed, but only after warning me not to allow myself to become too emotionally wrapped up in my work.

Athar laughed when I told her that. "Too late," she said.

I had the feeling she was not referring only to finding Cal and Selene.

—Giomanach

I didn't sleep at all during the rest of the night. Whenever I shut my eyes, images of Selene and Cal rose up, unbidden. By dawn I gave up and used my nervous energy to do the next week's math problems. The only thing that kept me from jumping out of my skin was the knowledge that the dark magick hadn't been focused on me.

I knew I had to tell Hunter about what I had experienced, and I didn't want to wait until the circle that night. I went out to the hall phone.

Mary K. walked by on her way to the bathroom. Her eyes widened when she saw me. "You're up early," she said. "You even have time to eat breakfast sitting down."

"I may be up, but I'm not awake," I warned her. I dialed Hunter's number, hoping he and Sky were early risers.

No answer. And no voicemail. I banged the phone down in frustration. Where the hell were they at this ridiculous hour?

Luckily Mary K. misinterpreted my mood as my usual morning crabbiness, so she didn't ask any questions. Stay calm, I ordered myself. Selene and Cal may be back, but you'll find some way to be ready for them.

Since I was already up, Mary K. and I set out for school early. She was stunned since she usually had to nag me into my car. I figured I'd use the opportunity to find out what the other members of Cirrus really thought about Hunter taking over.

I could feel Mary K.'s eyes on me while I drove. Did she sense my tension?

"Do you want to talk about it now?" she asked hesitantly.

I sighed. I felt bad for not telling her the full story. But I just wasn't up to it yet. I squeezed Das Boot into a snug parking space. "Soon, I promise. It's really . . . really hard.

Cal—he wasn't who I thought he was." Understatement of the year.

She sighed. "Is it the Rowlands's curse to have bad judgment when it comes to guys?" Mary K.'s ex-boyfriend, Bakker, had tried to force himself on her. I had been so furious that I'd shot witch fire at him without even realizing what I was doing. Still, that didn't stop her from taking him back. Or him from trying it again. Luckily she'd been stronger the second time. He was out of her life for good. I hoped.

"Mom did okay," I said.

"She wasn't a Rowlands," Mary K. pointed out darkly.

"True!" I said, and unbelievably, I giggled. Then we were hugging in the front seat of my demolition-derby car. "I'm glad you're my sister," I whispered.

"Back atcha," Mary K. said, and then her friend Jaycee ran up to the car, bundled in a Day-Glo-pink ski jacket.

"Mary K.," she cried excitedly, tapping the window. "You are *not* going to believe who Diane D'Alessio is going out with!"

"Just a sec," Mary K. told her. She turned back to me. "I'll talk to you later, okay?"

"Yep," I told her.

Mary K. and Jaycee hurried across the icy parking lot toward school. I grabbed my backpack and followed them.

Inside the redbrick building, I headed to the basement stairs, where our coven usually hung out on cold mornings. Jenna and Sharon were already there, along with Ethan. Matt, Jenna's ex, was nowhere to be seen, and neither was Robbie.

"Hey," I said.

Sharon looked up at me, relief evident in her expression. "Morgan! Are you all right? Robbie told us about Sunday night."

I sat down on the step beside Jenna. "Yeah, I'm okay. I guess."

Ethan shook his head. "That totally blew me away. I can't believe I missed all the signs that Cal was lethal."

"We all missed them," Sharon said, shuddering. Ethan put his arm around her shoulders.

Jenna tucked a strand of her pale blond hair behind her ear. "I feel so stupid. Like we were all taken in by a con artist or something. That the whole thing was just part of a plot to get at you."

"It's strange, but I can't help feeling that a lot of what he was doing was sincere," I said thoughtfully. Then I caught myself, wondering if I had a total victim personality or what. "Of course, he seemed pretty sincere about trying to kill me, too," I added briskly. "So now we know. Wicca definitely has a dark side, and Cal and Selene were practicing it."

Ethan stood up and shoved his hands into the pockets of his jeans. "You know, I like the part of Wicca that's about connecting with nature, understanding yourself. But this dark stuff scares me."

"I don't think any of us realized what we might be getting into when Cal started Cirrus," I said. "Now I guess we have to decide whether we want to go on with it."

"Did you hear that Hunter wants to lead the coven?" Jenna asked.

I nodded. "He told me last night. How do you all feel about it?"

"Weird," Jenna said. "I mean, we started with Cal. Being in the coven is so much connected with him for me. I don't know what it will be like. Plus it seems weird that Hunter would even want to lead us. He doesn't know us."

"He's worried about us being exposed to dark magick, and

he wants to make sure no one gets hurt. That's what he said, anyway," Sharon said. She smiled. "In his sexy English accent."

"Hey!" Ethan protested. "What about *my* sexy accent?"

"He does seem to know what he's talking about," Matt said. "He's been doing this a lot longer than we have. I know he's not much older than we are, but he seems . . . I don't know . . . more grown-up or something."

"It's just the accent," Ethan said, poking Sharon in the ribs. "It makes him seem older."

"Cut it out." Sharon wiggled away, laughing.

"You're right," I admitted. Hunter did seem older than his years. It probably had to do with all he'd been through. He'd had to grow up fast.

"I loved Cal's circles," Sharon said wistfully. "He was totally laid-back but at the same time encouraging."

"That last circle with him, I felt real magick," Jenna agreed. "Still, it might be interesting to see how Hunter handles things. For variety." The first bell rang, and she got to her feet. "All I know is, I'm not joining Sky's coven," she said. We all knew what she meant. Along with Bree, Raven Meltzer also belonged to Sky's coven. Raven had tried to seduce Matt, and Matt had pretty much gone for it. Hence the end of the four-year romance between Matt and Jenna.

Sharon said, "I think we ought to give him a chance."

"Yeah," Ethan said. "If we hate it, we can just quit."

For a moment, I envied them. If they didn't enjoy Wicca, they could drop it, the way you drop a boring after-school activity. I didn't have that option. Wicca had chosen me as much as I'd chosen it.

*　　　*　　　*

I'd hoped to get to Hunter and Sky's place early so that I could talk to Hunter about what I'd sensed the night before, but in the dark I missed the turn to his street and was out of Widow's Vale completely before I figured it out. By the time I pulled up in front of the house, it was already after seven, and everybody else's cars were parked against the curb. I wedged Das Boot in between Robbie's Beetle and Jenna's Corolla and started up the narrow path.

Hunter must have sensed me coming before I reached the porch. The front door opened, framing him in warm golden light. I caught my breath—it was so similar to the image of him in my dream, bathed in light, pushing back the darkness. I blinked to shake off the image. He watched me from the doorway, looking like one of those ads for an après-ski drink, and I suddenly felt self-conscious, as if I were about to slip and fall facedown on the walk.

"Welcome," he said.

"Morganita." Robbie came up behind him. "You've got to check this place out. It's very cool."

"I've been here before," I mumbled, oddly flustered.

Hunter stood aside to let me pass, and I walked into the living room. Sharon and Ethan were sharing an ottoman, leaning companionably against each other's backs. Jenna and Matt were in the armchairs, not looking at each other. Robbie sat down at one end of the blue velvet sofa and waved a hand at the seat next to him. I could sense that everyone was unsure about Hunter leading us, and I knew that Hunter sensed it, too.

"You know what's strange about this living room?" Robbie said. "There's no TV."

Hunter arched one blond eyebrow. "We don't have time

for it," he said. The implication was that neither should we. Not a great way to start.

"Is Sky here?" Jenna asked.

"No. She's out this evening," Hunter replied. He was wearing a deep-blue denim shirt, and worn black jeans hung loosely on his hips. I suddenly had a vivid flashback to the moment he'd almost kissed me, standing in the dark outside my house. That had been only three nights ago, but until this minute I'd forgotten about it.

I felt my cheeks burn. Where had that stray thought come from?

Hunter moved to stand in front of the hearth. "Welcome, everyone. I appreciate your showing up on a weeknight. I know this change is difficult. And I understand that despite the way things turned out with Cal, you liked the way he led Cirrus.

"My approach will inevitably be different," he went on. "But I'll try to see that Cirrus remains a coven where you feel comfortable, where you can be open with one another, where you can learn to safely draw on the power that lies within you, and where you will enter into a true connection with your magick."

Sharon smiled at that. But all I could think about was how with Cal the circles had seemed natural and comfortable. With Hunter it felt like we were getting the Wicca version of a Rotary Club speech.

"So," Hunter said, "let's begin. If you'll follow me, please . . ."

We followed him from the living room through a short hallway that I hadn't noticed when I'd been there before. It was lined with bookshelves that held a small collection of clothbound volumes. Through an arched doorway I could see into a small kitchen, where dried herbs and flowers hung from the ceiling.

At the end of the hall was a set of double wooden doors. Hunter opened them into a long, narrow room that was lit by candles and the glow of a wood-burning stove. The room ran the length of the house. Its back wall was covered with windows. A door led out to what seemed to be a deck. The windows rattled slightly, and I could hear the wind sighing through the trees.

An altar sat at one end of the room, holding more candles, a stick of burning incense, a shell, a dish of water in which purple blossoms floated, a pale blue crystal, and a stone sculpture of a woman. The sculpture was rough, the face barely defined, yet it was completely sensuous, a vision of the Goddess. You had only to look at it to know that it was made with love. I looked at Hunter. Had he sculpted it?

"Will you form a circle, please?" Hunter began. He sounded terribly proper and polite, very British. Once again I missed Cal with a pang and once again felt stupid and angry at myself for missing someone who had hurt me so badly.

I joined the others as Hunter drew a circle with white chalk around us. It was reassuring to feel Robbie on one side of me and Sharon on the other. I felt uneasy, though. I wondered if it was the threat of Selene and Cal or if it was Hunter. His presence always unsettled me, and being in a circle was so intimate. I wondered what it would be like to share this experience with him.

With the chalk Hunter traced four runes on each of the directional points. "I've chosen these runes specifically for our first circle together," he said. "Thorn is for new beginnings and opening gateways," he said, pointing to the rune at the east. "Beorc is a rune of growth. Ur is to create change and healing and strengthen all magick. Eolh is for protection."

I tried to quell the flutters in my stomach. What was my problem? Hunter hadn't done anything unusual so far.

"Did everyone bring the stones Cal gave out?" Hunter asked. When people nodded, he added, "Toss them into the middle of the circle, please."

Everyone but me pulled their stones out of their pockets. When they were all in a heap in the center of the chalk ring, Hunter drew a pentagram around them. At each of the five points he drew a symbol I didn't recognize.

"These sigils are from an older runic alphabet than the one we usually work with," he explained. "They're for protection and purification and will help strengthen our spell. We're going to use the circle itself to purify these stones. Now, have you all done the basic breathing exercises?"

Matt spoke up. "Cal taught us that."

"Then let's begin there," Hunter said. "May the circle of Cirrus always be strong."

We all joined hands, and I heard the familiar sound of Sharon's bracelets jingling against each other. I began to concentrate on my breathing, on pulling each inhalation deep into my stomach and then releasing it. Gradually I felt myself relax and become aware of the pattern of breathing within the circle. Hunter had the deepest, slowest breaths. Jenna, who was asthmatic, had the shallowest.

Hunter began to sing in a low voice. It was a simple chant in English, praising moon and sun, Goddess and God, asking them to be with us in our circle, to protect us from all evil intent and to guide us through the cycle of the seasons, the cycle of life. His voice was lilting, smooth and soft, yet with a core of strength. It resonated beautifully in the space. I never would have imagined that he could sing with such passion and simplicity. But for some reason, I couldn't hold on to the words. The others did, though, and as they sang together and we all moved widdershins, I saw their faces change. They were feeling something that I wasn't. A connection. Their voices gained power as some kind of energy surged through them. And I, the blood witch, the prodigy of Cirrus coven, felt nothing.

I became aware of Hunter's gaze on me. I closed my eyes, trying futilely to deepen my concentration, to snatch at the ethereal thread of magick that seemed to dance just out of reach. But I couldn't touch it, and finally, when I was almost weeping with frustration, Hunter slowed the circle and brought the song to an end. "Don't break the circle," he told us. "But everyone sit down."

We sat in place, our legs crossed.

"That was really good, everyone," Hunter said. His face glowed, his features relaxed in a way that I rarely saw, as if the circle was the place he felt most comfortable. It upset me that he could feel so at ease here in my coven while I, for the first time, felt like an outsider. He looked at each one of us in turn and then asked, "Do you want to share your thoughts?"

Ethan said, "That was . . . intense. The Wicca books talk about the Wheel of the Year. This time I felt like I could sort of . . . feel all of us traveling on it, our whole lives."

"Yeah," Matt said. "It was like I was both in this room and out there in the ravine."

"Me too." Robbie looked awestruck. "I felt like I was the wind in the trees."

Hunter looked at Sharon. "I didn't get anything cosmic," she admitted, sounding embarrassed. "I just felt how much my family cares about me. It was like I got this blast of mother-father love that I haven't been paying attention to lately."

Hunter smiled. "What makes you think that isn't cosmic?"

Robbie said, "What about you, Jenna?"

Jenna laughed softly. "I had a vision of myself being really *strong*."

It was my turn next, and I was dreading it. What had gone wrong? I wondered. Maybe Hunter was just the wrong person for me to be working with. Now I was going to have to say I hadn't felt anything, and everyone was going to wonder what was wrong with me, if I could only reach my power with Cal. I took a deep breath, trying to calm down.

"All right, then." Hunter got to his feet. "That was good work, everyone. Let's call it a night and meet again on Saturday."

I looked up, startled. He had skipped me!

When he walked over to blow out the altar candles, I followed him. "Do I not count?" I asked in a low voice. "Doesn't it matter what I felt?"

He glanced at me in surprise. "I could tell you didn't connect," he replied softly. "I thought you'd rather not talk about it. I'm sorry if I made the wrong assumption."

I couldn't think of a reply to that. It was the right assumption, in fact. It just bothered me, the way he could read me. I found it incredibly disconcerting.

He turned back to the others. "On Saturday we'll work

with the pentagram," he said. "Read up on it and spend some time visualizing it. See what it tells you."

I thought of Cal's pentacle necklace, and a shudder went through me.

"We can meet at my house," Jenna volunteered.

"Perfect," Hunter said. "Thank you all."

I knew I should seize the moment and tell him I needed to speak to him privately, but I just couldn't do it. I felt too off balance, too out of sorts. Before I'd made up my mind to do anything, Robbie came up and handed me my coat.

"So do you have a good book about pentagrams?" he asked as we walked out toward the cars.

"No," I said tiredly. "I don't seem to have anything right now."

7.
Intruder

April, 1986

Today I found Giomanach, all of three-and-a-half years old, hunched over a bowl of water, staring into it so intently that his eyes were almost crossing. When I asked him what he was doing, he told me he was scrying for his sister. Goddess, I was startled. We'd not told him that Fiona is carrying another child, yet he knew. He's amazingly quick.

I asked him if he'd seen anything, expecting him to say he hadn't. He's too young to scry. But he said he'd seen a little girl with dark hair and eyes. I smiled and told him we'd have to wait and see. But my leug told me our Alwyn will have red hair and green eyes like Fiona's, so I'm afraid the water lied to my boy. Unless it showed him its own riddling truth.

Then Giomanach smacked his hand down so the water spilled out of the bowl. I opened my mouth to scold him, but he

looked up at me with that little mischievous smile, and I hadn't the heart. He's like sunshine to me. After looking over my shoulder for two years. I'm finally beginning to accept that nothing is going to happen. that life can actually be this good.
—Maghach

I sat in Das Boot on Wednesday morning, thinking again about last night's circle. The truth was, part of me loved being the star pupil, the one who had off-the-charts power. In our coven, right from the start, I'd been the gifted one. It had made me feel special for the first time in my life. Was that over, too?

"Morgan?" a muffled voice called. "Morgan!"

I blinked and glanced up. My friend Tamara Pritchett was tapping on the window, her breath coming out in white puffs. "You're going to be late," she said as I rolled down the window. "Didn't you hear the bell?"

"Um . . . ," I mumbled. "Sorry. I was just thinking."

We walked to class together, and all the way there I was aware of the curious looks Tamara kept giving me. By now everyone knew that Cal was gone, that there had been a fire at his house. I'd told everyone who asked the standard story: that we'd broken up and I didn't know anything about the fire or where he was. But the people I'd been good friends with before Wicca came into my life, people like Tamara and Janice Yutoh, could tell there was a lot I wasn't saying.

I got through my morning classes, and then at lunch period I left school. I had an appointment for Das Boot at the body shop to get an estimate for the repairs. Unser's Auto Repair was off the highway on the outskirts of Widow's Vale. It was a big fenced lot, filled with cars, with a garage in the middle of it. With the exception of the Afton Enterprises gravel pit, which I passed about a quarter of a mile before Unser's, the road stretched out bleak and empty. I gave the gravel pit a glare as I drove past it, thinking of Practical Magick.

I pulled into the garage. Bob Unser, a gruff, gray-haired man in coveralls, wiped his hands on a rag and came over to the car as I got out. His big German shepherd, Max, bounded over, shoved his wet nose into my palm and licked it, then bounded away again. Max was technically a guard dog, but he was a total sweetheart. He and Bob both knew me pretty well. Being a genuine antique, Das Boot had had its share of problems, though nothing as major as this before.

Bob squinted at Das Boot's crumpled, scorched nose and smashed headlight. "What happened?"

"It kind of . . . collided with a building that was on fire."

He grunted. "That's original."

I huddled in my coat while he looked over Das Boot and made notes on a clipboard. "Let me call and get an estimate on the parts," he said. "Then I'll give you a total."

"Great." I had a feeling this repair was going to cost a fortune, and I wasn't sure how I was going to pay for it. I didn't want to put it on my parents' insurance and risk raising their rates.

Bob went into the little office, and I stayed in the garage. Max trotted back to my side, and I ran my hand through his thick coat. Then I felt the fur near his neck start to rise, and a low, rumbling growl filled the garage. I let go of him at once, wondering what was wrong.

Max swung his head toward the entrance of the garage. His growl deepened, and he loped outside. Then my own senses prickled. Something was out there. Something magickal.

My pulse rate picked up. I stood still, trying to get a better sense of the presence. It didn't feel human. Cautiously I stepped outside. Max stood on an icy patch of gravel a short distance from the garage, fur bristling and teeth bared. Then he began to race around the perimeter of the lot, barking furiously.

I cast out my senses and got feelings of stealth, concealment, malevolent power. Cold fear coursed through me, and my breath came fast as I traced the shape of Peorth in the air, the rune for revealing what is hidden. I visualized the rune, tracing it in my mind in bright red light until I felt its shape become a three-dimensional entity. Instinctively I began saying my power chant. "An di allaigh . . ."

There was a weird, whooshing noise, as if a whole flock of birds had started up from the ground at once. Something that felt like an ill wind brushed past me, making the tiny hairs on my arms stand up. I gasped. Max raced over to me, barking frantically. I saw nothing, but the air felt lighter, and I knew that the intruder was gone.

Bob walked out of the shop. "What's going on out here?" He frowned at Max, then at me. "What was all that noise about?"

I leaned against the car so he wouldn't see how I was shaking. "I guess Max heard something."

Max sat down in front of Bob and elaborated with short, eloquent barks.

"Okay, boy, okay." Bob was petting him now, comforting him. "We'll lock up good tonight."

We went back inside, and he handed me a written estimate for $750. That made me gasp again. "I'll have to special-order you a bumper and hood," he explained. "They don't make parts for this model anymore. I'll have to get them from a used-parts dealer in Pennsylvania. You call me and let me know when you're ready to go ahead."

I thanked him, barely even listening. Before I left I traced the rune Eolh on Max's forehead for protection. What had that mysterious presence been? Was it after me? Was it connected to the dark force I had felt the other night? Was it Cal or Selene?

Though the sun was shining brightly, I felt like a black veil had been pulled across the sky. Shivering, I got into my car and drove back to school.

Mary K. went to Jaycee's house after school, as she often did, so I drove straight home. I was still shaken up from the incident at the garage. I had no idea what it had been, but I didn't want to take any chances. I had felt something evil. If it was after me, I'd better start protecting myself fast.

In the empty house I went upstairs and took my birth mother's athame from its hiding place in the HVAC vent. Then I walked around the outside of my house, running the athame lightly over the clapboard siding. Hunter and Sky had placed runes of protection all around the house about two weeks ago. The athame revealed the magick signs to me, and I breathed a sigh of relief. They were still there and still glowing with potency.

Next I went up to my room and closed the door. I'd been planning to make an altar for some time, but now it seemed doubly urgent. If there really was someone or something after me, I needed to be as strong and sure in my magick as possible.

The problem was, the altar had to be somewhere my family wouldn't notice. Although my parents now seemed to realize that they couldn't prevent me from being a witch, there was no point in setting up an altar where they would see it and get upset.

I looked around my room. It wasn't big. There was no obvious place to set up an altar—certainly none that wouldn't be totally noticeable. I thought a moment and opened the door to my closet. It was a deep walk-in, with a long hanging rod running the length of it. I began taking clothes off the rod, laying shirts, dresses, jackets, and skirts on my bed. "Yuck," I said as a sundress with an enormous tropical flower print surfaced. It was time to give some things away.

When the closet was empty, I stared at the back of it. A small footlocker from when I went to summer camp sat on the floor. It had potential.

I rummaged in my dresser drawer for the length of plum-colored Irish linen that Aunt Eileen had brought back from her trip to Ireland. It covered the trunk perfectly, as if that's exactly what it had been woven for. Voilà. One altar.

Next I opened the junk drawer of my desk. I sorted through the crap until I found a small, perfect, pink-and-white scallop shell. I set it on one corner of the altar to represent water. On another I put a chunk of amethyst that had been among the crystals in Maeve's box of tools. That was for earth. On the remaining corners I set a candle for fire and a stick of incense for air. Of course, I wouldn't actually be able to light the candle or incense inside the closet. For that the altar would have to come out into my room. But I liked having all four elements in place.

I sat before my altar. It was pretty simple, as basic as you can get. Yet it felt right.

Something soft nudged me. Dagda. I ran my hand down his silky little back. "This is where we're going to invoke the Goddess," I explained. He purred as if in approval.

May I work strong, pure magick here, I said silently, spells of healing and wholeness.

And may they keep me safe, I couldn't help adding.

8.
Potential

Litha, 1991

Goddess, help us. How can we go on from here? We've lost everything—our home, our coven, our children. Our children.

It all came so suddenly. We'd both been feeling ill and out of sorts for weeks, but I didn't think much of it. Then, late yesterday evening, I was working in my study when I heard Fiona scream. I raced to her workroom and found her lying on the floor, her leug clutched in her hand. She had been scrying to find the source of her illness and had seen something hideous in the stone. She described it as a wave of darkness, like a swarm of black insects or a pall of smoke, sweeping over the land. "It was evil," she whispered. "It wants us. It's . . . searching for us. We've got to warn the others, and then we've got to go. Now. Tonight."

"Tonight? But—the children. Giomanach's got an herbology lesson tomorrow," I objected stupidly.

*The look she gave me broke my heart. "We can't take them,"
she said. "It wouldn't be safe. Not for them or for us. We've
got to leave them."*

*I argued, but in the end she convinced me that she was
right. The only hope for any of us was for Fiona and me to
disappear, to try somehow to draw the evil away from our
children.*

*Fiona left a frantic message for her brother Beck, who lives
in Somerset. Then we laid the strongest protections we could on
our house. I kissed my children as they slept, smoothing Alwyn's
tangled red curls, pulling the covers back up over Linden. Last
of all I stood by Giomanach, watching the rise and fall of his
chest. I tucked my leug under his pillow, where he'd find it in
the morning.*

And then, once again, I abandoned my children.

—Maghach

I left a note for my mom saying that I'd be back for dinner, then drove over to Hunter's house. As much as being
around him upset me, I realized Hunter needed to know
about the dark presence I'd sensed at Unser's and the dark
magick I had felt on Monday night. He might be able to tell
me what it was, where it had come from, how I could protect myself from it effectively.

I started up the narrow path. Even in daylight it was hard
to be sure that there was a house tucked away behind all the
trees. The porch was even ricketier than it had seemed at

night. A post was missing from the railing, and the stairs had a split tread.

I reached the door and hesitated. Should I knock? I suddenly felt reluctant to bring my troubles to this particular door.

I chickened out. I'd turned and started off the porch when I heard the door open behind me. "Morgan," Hunter's voice said.

Caught. I turned to face him and felt myself blush. "I should have called first. Maybe this isn't a good time."

"It's fine," he said. "Come in."

Inside there was no sign of Sky. I settled myself in one of the living-room armchairs. The house was as cold as it had been last night, the fire in the little fireplace giving off hardly any warmth at all. I was shivering, growing more uncomfortable by the second. This had been a bad idea.

"So," Hunter said as he sat across from me. "Why are you here?"

To my surprise, I blurted, "I didn't feel anything at our circle last night. I'm the one who always gets swept away, but . . . Everyone else was transported, but I didn't get anything. I don't know if Cirrus is right for me anymore."

"Wicca isn't about getting things," Hunter said.

"I know that," I said defensively. "It's just—it's just that it doesn't usually happen to me." I studied his face, wondering how much to confide in him. "It scared me," I admitted. "Like my powers would be gone forever." A thought occurred to me. "Did you do something to damp down my power during the circle in any way?"

He raised his eyebrows. "If I were trying to control your

power, you'd have known it. And it's not something I would do unless it were an extreme emergency."

"Oh." I sank back into the chair.

He crossed a booted foot over his knee. He tapped it a few times. "Perhaps . . . my style doesn't bring out your potential."

He sounded disappointed. In me, I wondered, or in himself? "Everyone else, it worked for them," I said grudgingly. "They really liked how you did things."

His face brightened, making him look more like an ordinary teenager. Extraordinarily handsome, maybe, but less intense. "They did? I'm glad. I haven't been that nervous since . . . well, never mind." He pressed his lips together as if he wanted to make sure he didn't say anything else. He looked almost startled—as if he hadn't meant to say those words aloud.

"You were nervous?" I couldn't help enjoying that. "The mighty Hunter?"

Hunter leaned forward, gazing into the hearth. "Don't you think I know how highly you all thought of Cal? Especially you. I knew no one really wanted me taking over. And a part of me thought: Well, maybe they're right. Maybe I can't lead a circle as well as he did. God knows he's more at ease with people than I'll ever be."

I stared at him, stunned to hear him admit to so much vulnerability. I thought back to times when I'd watched Cal move from one clique at school to another, fitting in wherever he went. It was part of what had made him so good at manipulating people—he could present them with what they wanted to see. And what made it so powerful was that at some level, it was real. Hunter, on the other hand, could only be himself.

He and I had that in common.

A sadness clouded his clear green eyes. "I always thought my father would be there when I took over as a coven leader. It feels strange to take the step without him."

I nodded, aware of another connection we had. "Like my trying to learn about my birthright without my birth parents. I feel like something is missing."

"Yes," Hunter agreed. "Without Dad, being coven leader is all that more daunting."

"What made you decide to do it, then?" I asked.

He gave me a sudden, lopsided grin, gazing up at me from under a shock of pale hair. "The thought that *you* might try to lead them. I couldn't risk that."

If that was a joke, I didn't find it particularly funny. "Hey, I didn't come here to be insulted."

"Oh, stop." He laughed. "I didn't mean it as an insult. I only meant that you're a bit of a loose cannon because you've got all this power and no training. It's not an incurable condition."

"Glad to know it's not terminal," I muttered.

He looked at me more seriously now. "Morgan, listen to me. You have so much potential—it's very exciting, I know. But you've got to learn how to rein in and focus your power. For your own good as much as anything else. All that power makes you like a beacon. You're a walking target."

Abruptly I remembered the real reason I'd come here. I sat forward in my chair.

"There's something I need to tell you about," I said. I

described the dark force I'd felt after my dream and then again at the garage. "I tried to get it to reveal itself by drawing Peorth, but it just sort of evaporated," I said. "Do you have any idea what it was?"

He was frowning. "This is not good. It could have been another witch, cloaking him or herself. It sounds more like some sort of a taibhs, a dark spirit, though."

"The first time, when I sensed it in the middle of the night, I had the impression that whatever it was, it wasn't aimed at me," I said. "But after what happened at the garage, I'm not so sure. Do you think it's been following me?"

"You would have sensed that, I think." Hunter got to his feet, went to the window, and peered out into the trees that surrounded the house. "But we've got to assume that it wasn't coincidence, either. It was looking for you. And it found you."

"Did Selene send it? Or . . . Cal?" I asked in a low voice, not really wanting to know the answer.

"More likely Selene," Hunter said. "To her your power is an irresistible lure, almost as much as Belwicket's tools are. If she can't coerce you to join her group, she wants to absorb your power. It would increase her own to the point where she'd be practically invincible."

My skin crawled. I thought of David, saying that we had to take Selene's intentions into account as well as her actions. Maybe he was right, but her intentions sounded pretty awful in themselves. "They're really evil, aren't they?" I asked. "Selene and . . . and Cal?"

He took some branches from the box of kindling, snapped them in half, and added them to the fire. "Cal . . . is

his mother's creation. I don't know if I'd call him evil."
Glancing up, he gave me that quick grin again. "Besides, that's
not a nice thing to say about one's own kin, is it?"

I grinned back. Hunter did have a sense of humor, I realized. It was just an offbeat one.

"As for Selene," Hunter went on, getting serious again.
"She's ambitious and ruthless. She studied with Clyda Rockpel."

I shook my head, indicating that I didn't know the name.

"Clyda Rockpel was a Welsh Woodbane who was legen-
darily vicious. She's said to have murdered her own daughter
to enhance her power. And it's certainly true that wherever
Selene goes, witches tend to disappear or die. Destruction
seems to follow in her wake. Yes, I would agree that she is
truly evil."

I felt a wave of pity for Cal. With a mother like that, he'd
never really had a choice. Or a chance.

As if he'd read my mind, Hunter said in a quiet voice,
"Poor Cal." His eyes met mine, and I was startled by the
depth of compassion in them.

We stared at each other, and then we were both suspended in a strange, timeless moment. I felt like I was falling
into Hunter's gaze, and again I remembered the night when
he'd almost kissed me. Of the profound connection I'd felt
with him, the lightness I'd experienced when he and I had
done tàth meànma, the intense sharing of minds I thought of
as the Wiccan mind meld.

I wanted to feel Hunter's mouth on mine, his arms
around me. I wanted to kiss away that sadness, all that had
happened to him before we'd met. To tell him that his father
would be proud of him if only he could be here. I could feel

him wanting to do the same for me; I could sense him aching to stroke my face until he had wiped away all the tears I'd shed over Cal.

Then I blinked. What was I *thinking?* Here I was, talking to my ex-boyfriend's half brother and fantasizing about making out with him. Was I insane?

"I—I've got to go home," I said.

A faint flush had risen under Hunter's clear, pale skin. "Right," he said, standing up. He cleared his throat. "Wait just a moment. I've got some books for you."

He strode into the hallway and began pulling books off the shelves. "Here," he said, his voice back to its usually proper tone. "An advanced compendium of runic alphabets, Hope Whitelaw's critique of Erland Erlandsson's numerological system, and a guide to the properties of stones, minerals, and metals. Start with these, and when you've finished them, we'll talk about them. Then I'll give you more."

I nodded, not trusting myself to speak. When I took Hunter's books, I was careful to not allow our hands to touch.

Outside, the late afternoon sky was a harsh, glaring white. I drove home in a daze, my mind whirling, barely noticing the cold at all.

9.
Almost Normal

It happened again this afternoon. Just the way it did that other night. We were talking—talking about how to protect her, actually—and then, suddenly, I looked at her and it was as if I'd found an entire universe within her eyes. And I wanted so badly just to touch her, to kiss her mouth . . . I can't stop thinking about her. She moves me so strongly, so strangely. I've never felt like this before.

I'm an idiot. She can barely stand me.

—Giomanach

Thursday and Friday, I worked really hard on keeping things normal. I went to school. I talked to my friends. I worked at my mom's office—I'd made a deal with my parents in which they'd front me the money for my car repairs in exchange for me getting all my mom's real estate listings entered into the computer. I cheered when the news came that Aunt Eileen and Paula had closed on their house and that they would start moving in over the weekend. I tried not to think about Cal. Or Hunter. Or the bad news about Practical Magick. Or dark forces that might be out to get me. I made it through the days like other teenage girls.

On Saturday, Robbie picked me up in his red Beetle. By now everyone in the coven had heard about Practical Magick closing, and Robbie had suggested a trip over there to see if there was anything we could do to help. I didn't think there was, but I was glad to go, anyway.

"So, how'd it go last night?" I asked as I buckled my seat belt. I knew that Robbie had gone out with Bree. It was a new direction for their age-old friendship.

Robbie shook his head, gazing through the windshield. "Same as before. We hung out, watched a video. Then we made out, and it was great. Fantastic. But the second I tried to talk about how I felt, she got all squirrelly." He grinned. "But this time I had the sense to shut up and kiss her again before she kicked me out of her house."

I laughed. "Quick thinking."

The fact was, Robbie had been in love with Bree for years. But Bree was gorgeous, while Robbie . . . well, he'd been a pizza face. It had made him afraid to approach her. Then, in trying out my newfound power, I'd made a potion to clear up the acne that for years had obliterated his looks. The potion had worked and kept on working in an almost frightening way. The scars had disappeared completely, and then his poor vision had improved, to the point where he no longer wore the thick glasses that he'd had ever since I'd known him. Without the acne or the glasses, he turned out to be amazingly good-looking and was now considered a major hottie at school.

With his new looks, Robbie had found the courage to go after Bree. But the results so far were uneven. They weren't exactly seeing each other but were definitely more than friends. On Robbie's side, it was love. For Bree . . . it was impossible to tell. Even back when we told each other everything, she'd always been hard to figure out when it came to relationships.

Thinking about Bree, I felt another pang of loss. With all that had happened to me in such a short amount of time, it was painful to not be able to confide in her. But the wounds were still too fresh. Maybe, just maybe, with Cal gone, we could begin to be friends again. I hoped so.

Robbie and I talked about Practical Magick's problems for the rest of the drive. Robbie's brow creased as he hunted for a parking space in front of the store. "There's something I don't get," he said. "I mean, we've got you, David, Alyce, Hunter, and Sky—that's five blood witches. And I assume you'd all like Practical Magick to stay open. Why can't you just all do a spell together so David hits the lottery or something?"

"I'm sure that kind of thing isn't allowed under Wiccan law," I said gloomily. "Otherwise David and Alyce would have done it already."

"That's a drag," Robbie said. He squeezed into a space behind a minivan, and we started for the store.

I nodded, but I couldn't help thinking—there must be some kind of spell to increase wealth. After all, going by the listings I'd seen in my mom's office, Selene Belltower's property must be worth at least a million dollars. And although

Cal had told me that Selene's employers had transferred her to Widow's Vale, I never had found out what she supposedly did for a living. I had a feeling her money didn't come through any of the usual channels.

Robbie pushed open the door, and I followed him into the store. I was stunned by Alyce's reception.

"Morgan!" she called. Her eyes were sparkling, her cheeks were pink, and she sounded almost giddy. "Robbie! I'm so glad to see you. I have excellent news!"

"What happened?" I asked.

"It's almost unbelievable. Stuart Afton has forgiven Rosaline's debt!" Alyce said.

"What?" I practically shrieked. "How did that happen?"

"Do rich people really do that?" Robbie asked.

"Apparently this one does," Alyce said, laughing. "Afton called David late last night to say he'd made a sudden windfall on the stock market and he'd decided to pass on some of his good fortune. I suppose it's the Yule spirit."

David stepped out from the little back room. "Have you heard?"

"Alyce was just telling us," I answered. "It's too good to be true."

David gave a faint smile. "It is rather surprising," he said.

"So the deal with the bookstore chain is off?" Robbie asked.

"That's right," David said. "And the upstairs tenants can stay, with their same rent."

"Best of all, Practical Magick stays," Alyce added. "We're throwing a party here tonight to celebrate. I was just going to start making calls to invite all of you, in fact. We want everyone to come—Wiccans, Catholics, Buddhists, atheists, you name it."

This was such great news. Even the idea of dark forces around couldn't keep me from a celebratory mood. "We'll be here," I promised.

"Uh, Morgan." Robbie elbowed me. "Hunter scheduled a circle tonight, remember?"

I'd forgotten, in fact. My stomach did a flip-flop at the thought of seeing Hunter again.

"I already spoke to Hunter. He's going to reschedule," Alyce said. She was practically giggling. "You don't get a gift like this every day, and we must give it a proper welcome. I've already arranged for The Fianna to play. It was the first thing I did when I heard the news." The Fianna was a hot Celtic pop band. Mary K. and I had tried to get tickets to one of their concerts last spring, and they had been totally sold out.

I glanced at David, who was methodically counting Tarot decks. Compared to Alyce's high-energy happiness, he seemed subdued. Then I remembered that this positive outcome came from a loss—the death of David's aunt. Perhaps now that the immediate crisis about the building was over, he had more time to actually feel his grief. Well, as Wicca teaches, everything is cyclical. Life leads to death leads to rebirth.

I wondered what kind of cycle I was in with Hunter. Annoyance leads to dreaming of kissing him to . . . irritation again?

"So what non-Wiccans are going to be at this party?" Mary K. asked as we waited for Das Boot's windshield to defrost. I'd come home that afternoon to find her so down about her breakup with Bakker that I'd talked her into coming with me to the Practical Magick party. Mary K. felt pretty much the same way that my parents did about Wicca, so she'd been reluctant—until I mentioned that The Fianna was going to play.

"The Fianna?" she'd gasped. "For real?"

After that she couldn't say no.

I wasn't just being nice by inviting her; I needed her support. I've never been the most comfortable person at a party. And knowing that Hunter would be there made me even more nervous.

I blew on my fingers to warm them up. "I'm not sure who'll be there," I said. "Probably the people who live above the shop. Plus you'll know Robbie and Bree and the other kids from school. They're Wiccans, but they're still people you've known forever."

I glanced at Mary K. She was wearing a short brown wool skirt and a russet-colored sweater. Citrine earrings sparkled against her auburn hair. As usual she looked perfect—neither too casual nor too dressy, just undeniably pretty.

"Well, you look great," she said, sounding uncharacteristically nervous.

On her advice, I had worn a lavender sweater, a long forest green skirt, an amethyst necklace, and brown lace-up boots. Did I really look good? Except when I was making magick, I usually felt depressingly plain. I'm five-foot-six, completely flat chested, with boring, medium-brown hair and what my mother calls "a strong nose." I mean, I'm not revolting or anything, but I'm not pretty.

At least, I was never pretty until Cal. Cal himself was so beautiful, he could have had any girl he wanted—and he chose me. Of course, he had chosen me for awful reasons, but in spite of that I didn't believe he'd totally faked the way he looked at me, touched me, kissed me. It seemed like I'd become beautiful. Now, without him, I felt plain again.

Mary K. fiddled with her seat belt and turned to me. "So . . . what happened with you and Cal? I mean, the real story."

My fingers tightened on the steering wheel. I took a deep breath. Then I finally told her everything that had happened the day of the fire. Everything I hadn't told my parents.

"Oh my God," was all she could say when I was done. "Oh my God, Morgan."

"You know, I owe you an apology for being so judgmental about you and Bakker," I told her. "I guess I expected you to handle the whole situation according to a simple, rational formula: Bakker hurts Mary K.; Mary K. dumps Bakker."

"That's how it should have been." Mary K.'s voice was so quiet, I could barely hear her. "I can't believe I gave him another chance."

"Two weeks ago I couldn't understand that," I said slowly, my thoughts forming my words. "But feelings don't work rationally. I did the same thing. All last week I knew things were wrong with Cal. But I didn't want to believe he could hurt me, even after he used his magick against me."

"He'd done it before?"

"The night before my birthday." The night we almost killed Hunter, I thought. Mary K. didn't need to know that part. I swallowed hard. "Cal—put a binding spell on me. I couldn't move. It was like I was drugged."

"Oh, great. All these things you're telling me really make me want to walk into a room full of witches." Mary K. peered out through her window as I pulled into a parking spot down the block from Practical Magick. "Is it too late to turn around and go home?"

"Yes. It's too late." I smiled and shut off the engine, but Mary K. just sat there, tugging her glove off and then on again. When she spoke, she sounded young and vulnerable.

"I appreciate what you said about me and Bakker. And I know that Wicca and your—your birth mother mean a lot to you. But all this witch stuff—it scares me. Especially when you tell me what's happened to you because of it."

I sighed. Maybe I'd told her too much.

"That's why it's so important to me that you come to this party," I tried to explain. "I want you to meet these people, to see that they're not all weird or scary or evil. I don't want to have to hide what I am. Please, Mary K. If you're really uncomfortable, we won't stay. I promise."

She looked down at her lap. After a moment she nodded.

"Okay," I said, trying to sound cheery. "Let's party."

10.
The Party

July, 1991

We are in Bordeaux, staying with Leandre, a Wyndenkell cousin of Fiona's. Fiona is not well. She says it's only a chill she caught during the channel crossing, but I'm afraid it's something more serious. For a week now she's had a fever every night, and none of the usual remedies seem to help it. I'm almost ready to suggest that she go to a doctor of western medicine.

I went out today and hunted through the fields until I found a chunk of quartz the size of my fist. It's not as good as obsidian, but I think it will serve. I'm going to scry for our children, our town, our coven. I feel heavy with dread at the thought of what I might see.

—Maghach

Mary K. wasn't the only one who was nervous. I felt flutters in my stomach as we walked up the block toward the store. It had occurred to me that I was going to have to walk into a room full of people who all probably knew exactly what had happened with me and Cal. I pictured the talk stopping and all eyes turning toward me and Mary K. the minute we opened the door. My pace slowed to a halt.

Mary K. looked at my face. "Want to go home?" she asked shrewdly.

I swallowed. "No. Come on."

As it turned out, our entrance hardly attracted any notice at all. I stood by the glass doors, peeling off my gloves and gathering my courage. The party was already in full swing. Practical Magick was lit with candles and tiny white Christmas lights, and fragrant pine boughs decked the molding. Shelves had been moved into the nonbook half of the store so a platform stage could be set up. A cloth printed with Celtic knots was draped over the counter and covered with platters of food.

Alyce, wearing a long blue velvet dress, was the first to greet us. "Morgan," she said, folding me into a hug. "You look wonderful. I'm so glad you made it. And this is . . . ?"

"My sister, Mary K."

"Welcome," she said, clasping both of Mary K.'s hands in hers. "What a pleasure to meet you." Mary K. smiled; it was impossible not to respond to Alyce's warmth.

Alyce waved us in. "It's crowded already," she warned. "There's a coatrack set up against the back wall, cold drinks by the stockroom door, and hot apple cider on the little table by the Books of Shadows."

"Are The Fianna really playing?" asked Mary K.

"They are. They're in the back room, going over their set list."

"How did you ever get them?" Mary K. was clearly awestruck.

"Connections," Alyce told her. "The lead guitarist is my nephew. Would you like to meet them?"

My sister's eyes widened. "Are you serious?"

"Now's your chance." Alyce slipped an arm through Mary K.'s and led her behind the counter and into the back room.

I surveyed the other guests. It *was* crowded. I spotted the elderly couple from upstairs holding hands and beaming happily. Even from across the room, I could sense their relief. I felt a rush of pleasure, knowing that some problems had quick and happy solutions.

Sharon and Ethan were standing near an aluminum tub filled with ice and canned drinks, their heads bent toward each other. Jenna, wearing a silky slip dress with a cropped cardigan, was chatting animatedly to a guy who'd been in the shop the other day. He was laughing at something she said, and I noticed her ex, Matt, watching them. From the way Jenna cast a subtle glance in Matt's direction, I could tell she enjoyed knowing that Matt was watching her flirt.

Things are getting more and more complicated, I thought. I glanced around, looking for Hunter. I almost missed him because he was kneeling down in deep conversation with a little boy I recognized as the four-year-old son of the other tenant, Lisa Winston. The little boy seemed to be explaining something very important to Hunter, and Hunter was nodding seriously. Then Hunter said something, and the boy laughed with delight. Hunter must have felt my eyes on him because he suddenly glanced my way. I felt my heart catch; was it nerves?

Hunter went back to talking to the boy, and I was wondering if I should go join them when I heard someone say my name behind me.

"Morgan, isn't it?" I turned to see a middle-aged woman with salt-and-pepper hair in a thick French braid. She looked familiar, yet I couldn't place her.

"I'm Riva. I met you once at Selene's. I'm part of Starlocket," she explained. "I heard about what Selene and Cal tried to do to you," she added, staring at me.

"Oh," I said. This was just what I'd been afraid of. I felt like a zoo exhibit and wished desperately that she'd just go away and leave me alone.

"I couldn't believe it," she went on. "I had no idea Selene was mixed up with dark magick. I promise you, if any of us had known, we wouldn't have let her lead us."

"Thanks," I said awkwardly. "That's good to know."

She nodded and moved on to talk with another woman I recognized from Starlocket.

The mention of dark magick made me think again of the presence I'd felt at home and at the garage. I had checked to be sure that the protective sigils that Sky and Hunter had left at the house were still there, and it was reassuring that they were. Knowing that I had my altar set up also gave me something approaching peace of mind. Maybe I should find a book on altar magick, I thought. At least it would give me something to do besides standing here like a dork.

As I moved to the book section of the store, I felt a cold draft and turned to see the front door open.

"We're here!" Raven Meltzer announced from the open doorway. "The party can start now!" She strode into the store, Bree and Sky following her.

Raven took the prize for most outrageous outfit—no surprise there. She hadn't even bothered to wear a coat; she probably didn't want anything to spoil her dramatic entrance. Her black leather bustier showed off both the circle of flames tattooed around her belly button and a generous amount of cleavage. She wore tight black leather hip huggers, heavy-soled biker boots, hematite bracelets on her wrists, silver chains around her throat, and glittery eye shadow that went clear out to her temples. She'd put blue highlights in her dyed black hair. Catching sight of Matt, she gave him a smile and then ran her tongue over her lips in a slow, deliberate way. He flushed heavily.

As Bree shrugged off her heavy coat, Robbie stepped up to take it from her. But he was too late; a guy I knew from English class had already grabbed it, and Bree was thanking him sweetly, touching his arm. She was looking even more glamorous than usual in a slim coppery sheath of a dress.

Sky was as beautiful as Bree and Raven but in a completely different way. She was more subdued, more contained, in a pair of black jeans and a midnight blue camisole that set off her pale complexion and dark eyes. Those eyes never left Raven. She watched her in fascination, with yearning. I had been shocked to discover that Sky had a serious thing for Raven; they were so different. Maybe for Sky that was part of the attraction.

I sighed. Matt wanted Raven but sort of still wanted Jenna, too. Raven wanted to tease Matt and maybe Sky as well. Sky wanted Raven. Robbie wanted Bree, who only wanted boys she didn't have to take seriously. And I still wanted Cal, who had tried to kill me. Except when I wanted Hunter, whom I couldn't stand . . . Suddenly the idea of joining a convent sounded very appealing.

I snorted a laugh. Could witches even join convents? Well, this was one mess that I couldn't blame on Wicca, I realized. Wicca might have brought us together and intensified our feelings, but this little soap opera had high school hormones written all over it. In a weird way, the normalcy of these huge problems felt comforting.

And here I was, back to feeling my normal wallflower self.

Bree caught my eye and gave me a cautious little grin. She knew how uncomfortable I was in social situations. I had always counted on her to get me through them. I smiled back.

To my surprise, she walked over to me. "Hey, Morgan. That skirt looks great on you."

"Mary K. put this outfit together for me," I confessed.

Bree laughed, not meanly. "I figured." We stood side by side for a moment, looking out at the crowd. Then she asked quietly, "Is it hard for you, being here without Cal?"

I glanced at her, startled. I hadn't expected anything that direct. But as I met her gaze, I wanted so badly to reconnect with her.

"Everything feels hard with him gone," I said. My words tumbled out. "I miss him all the time. I feel like such a moron. It's like something out of a tabloid: High School Witch Grieves for Would-be Murderer."

"You're not a moron," she said. "You really cared about him. And—and maybe in some twisted way, he really cared about you, too."

I nodded numbly. I knew that it had been hard for her to say that. She had wanted Cal for herself. And it made me feel less like an idiot to think that he did care for me, even just a little.

Bree hesitated. "You know, I've been thinking about the way he played us."

I froze. Bree was treading on dangerous ground here.

"What I'm saying is . . ." She looked massively uncomfortable, then plunged ahead. "I think Cal deliberately slept with me, knowing it would set us against each other."

I gaped at her. "What?"

"He wanted to isolate you," she explained. "Come on, Morgan. You and I were best friends. We talked about everything. We trusted each other." Bree's voice started to quaver, and I could see her fighting to steady it. "Cal was trying to take you over, to control you completely. It would make sense for him to make sure he was the only one you talked to, the only one you really trusted. If he split us up, you'd be more dependent on him."

In a flash of sickening clarity, I realized she was right. I felt like I'd just been punched in the stomach. Every time I thought I'd faced the worst about Cal, I found more—new and deeper layers of deception on his part, blindness on mine.

"He pitted us against each other. He used us both," Bree said.

I nodded, unable to speak, seeing more layers falling away.

But as I stood there, trying to process it all, it occurred

to me that even if Bree was right about Cal, no one had forced her to do the cruel things she'd done to me. Maybe things were mending between us, but they could never go back to what they had once been. We'd never trust each other the way we used to. I felt incredibly sad.

"What happened to David?" Bree said, pulling my attention back to the room.

"What?" I asked.

She nodded toward the counter. David was dipping a carrot stick into some hummus. His left hand was wrapped in a white gauze bandage.

"I don't know," I said. "Let's go find out."

Before I could move, Mary K. emerged from the back room and, to my astonishment walked up onto the platform and took the mike. "Excuse me. Could I have everyone's attention, please?" she said. When the room was quiet, she announced with a huge grin, "I'm pleased to introduce The Fianna!"

Practical Magick erupted into applause as The Fianna made their way onto the stage. They were four skinny young guys and a wisp of a girl with short red hair. She launched into an a cappella verse in a voice that was positively haunting. It reminded me of Hunter's voice when he sang the chant in our circle, a voice drawn out of the world of our ancestors, a pure, shimmering thread that connected us to the past.

I jumped when I heard Hunter's voice behind me. "I need to talk to you," he said quietly.

Bree gave me a questioning look and then moved to rejoin Sky across the room.

"Not here," Hunter said. Taking my elbow, he led me through the crowded room and out the door.

"It's freezing out here," I complained, crossing my arms over my nonexistent chest. "And I want to hear The Fianna."

"Morbid Irish ballads later," he said. "Believe me, there are plenty more where those came from." He opened the door to Sky's green car. "Get in."

I ducked into the passenger seat, muttering, "Do you always have to order me around?"

He grinned. "It's the cold," he said. "Don't have time for the niceties. Don't want you freezing in that pretty outfit." He shut my door, then climbed into the driver's seat.

Flustered at hearing the word *pretty* come out of his mouth in reference to me, I sat there in silence.

He turned on the heat, then rubbed his hands to warm them up. "I went to that field. Where you thought the first dark presence might have been."

"Wh-what did you find out?" I wasn't sure if I wanted to hear his answer.

He shook his head. "I don't think it was Selene."

"Really?" My heart returned to its normal rhythm. But then it sped up again as I asked, "But then who? What?"

Hunter let out a sigh. "That's just it. I'm not entirely sure. There was a dark ritual performed there—you were right about that." He gave me a quick glance. I knew my abilities as a beginning witch still surprised him. "But the traces I found of the ritual suggested to me that whoever performed it was someone who had to work quite hard to conjure power."

"What kind of traces?" I was fascinated in spite of myself.

"Blood, among other things," Hunter said, and I gasped. "One of the ways to summon a dark spirit is with a blood offering. But that isn't something Selene would need to do."

I shut my eyes. "Do you think it was Cal?" I asked in a low voice.

"It could be. But why he'd do work like that without Selene . . . well, it just doesn't add up."

I felt a tiny flicker of hope. Maybe Cal had left Selene. Maybe he was on his own because he'd come back to be with me. I doused that flame by reminding myself that it had been dark magick that I had felt, which would mean that Cal would still be incredibly dangerous.

I shivered, and it wasn't with cold. "If it's not Cal and Selene, who could it be? Who would perform a dark magick ritual?" I asked. I glanced at the door to Practical Magick, wondering if the wayward witch was inside. Among us. And what he or she would do next.

Hunter didn't respond. He looked straight ahead.

"What?" I demanded, a prickle of foreboding making the hairs on my arms stand up. "What aren't you telling me?" I was so sick of secrets and lies that my voice was louder than I had planned.

Hunter's jaw tightened, then he turned to face me. "You won't like this. I don't, either. But hasn't it occurred to you that Practical Magick was saved just in the nick of time? Don't you find it convenient that Stuart Afton has forgiven this huge debt, out of the blue?"

I stared at him. "Alyce said the guy had a windfall," I explained. "If I suddenly came into lots of money, I'd be generous, too."

Hunter smirked at me. "You, clearly, are not a business-man."

"It's not possible," I snapped. "Are you really suggesting that David and Alyce used some kind of dark magick to get Stuart Afton to cancel the debt?"

"Not necessarily Alyce," Hunter said. "But David, yes—I think it's possible. Did you notice the bandage on his hand?"

"What about it?" I asked, nonplussed.

"Remember the blood I found in the field?"

"Huh?" At first I didn't understand what he was trying to say. But then I got it, and it was so absurd, I let out a sharp laugh. "Oh, please. Are you saying David hurt his hand making a blood offering to a dark spirit? Come on! There are a dozen other ways he could have hurt himself. Did you even ask him about it?"

"Not yet," Hunter admitted.

"I can't believe you're thinking this way," I said. "I mean, we *know* Cal and Selene use dark magick, and we know the magick was done in a place Cal used to go to. Why are you even bringing David into it? Why do you have to be suspicious about *everything?*" I was starting to get worked up again. "Why can't good news just be good news?"

Hunter was silent. The door to Practical Magick opened as a couple entered, and the singer's voice drifted into the night. She was singing a joyful song of coming spring, and I was suddenly impatient to share in that pleasure, not sit out here listening to Hunter's ridiculous theories. I flung open the car door and hurried back inside.

The Fianna played for almost an hour, and practically everyone in the room danced. Mary K. even tugged me out onto the floor for a song. I ignored Hunter as best I could and noticed he left early.

After another hour or so, people began to filter out. Mary K. and I got our coats. As she went to say good night to the band, David joined me at the cider table.

"Did you enjoy yourself?" he asked.

I nodded and gave him a smile. "What happened to your hand?" I asked.

David shrugged. "My knife slipped as I was trimming pine boughs."

Ha, I thought. Wait until I tell Hunter. So much for his suspicions.

Mary K. returned, proudly displaying her autographed Fianna CD. "I can't wait until Jaycee gets a load of this," she declared as we headed for the car.

"So now do you believe that all Wiccans aren't evil and weird?" I asked Mary K.

"I'll say one thing for them," she answered. "They know how to throw a party. I still can't believe I met The Fianna!" She clutched the CD to her chest.

As I kicked Das Boot into gear, she went on. "It's just that . . . well, Wicca isn't my way. And the fact that the church is against it doesn't help," she added more quietly. Mary K. wasn't as religious as Mom or our aunt Maureen, but she did basically believe in what Catholicism taught. "I have to say I was never totally comfortable in there."

I nodded. I'd already pretty much known that my sister felt like this. But to hear it confirmed so baldly was painful. So that was it, I thought. The essence of my identity, the core of who I was, was the very thing that created an unbridgeable gap between me and my family.

We drove the rest of the way home in silence.

11
Hunted

July, 1991

In Milan now. A close escape. It was my scrying, I think, that alerted the evil to our presence in Bordeaux.

First I sought our children and found them, as I had prayed they would be, safe with Beck. Then I asked my quartz to help me see our coven, and I saw. Oh, Goddess.

I saw the utter devastation of our town, the swathe of burnt houses, charred cars, blackened tree trunks whose branches seemed to claw at the sky in their agony. . . . Nothing, it seemed, was spared. Nothing except our house. It stood there, the mellow brick darkened by a pall of ash but otherwise untouched.

Then, from our bedroom, I heard Fiona screaming. I ran in and found her sitting upright in bed, her eyes wild.

"It's coming," she cried. "It's found us. We have to go!"
She's calling me. More later.
—Maghach

My dad was in the kitchen when I came down the next morning, wearing his usual winter outfit of khakis, button-down shirt, and knit vest. He was peeling potatoes for dinner, then dropping them into a bowl of ice water. My dad has a thing about preparing far in advance.

"Your cat would like you to feed him," my dad greeted me.

Sure enough, Dagda was sitting on the floor next to his bowl, looking up with a hopeful expression. He wound himself around my ankles, arching his little back against my hand. I bent and picked up the dish.

"How was the party?" my dad asked as I spooned canned food into Dagda's bowl.

"Okay," I replied. Disturbing, I added silently. I went to the fridge and scanned for food.

"Morgan, don't just stand there with the door open," he admonished me.

"Sorry," I said. I grabbed a box of waffles and shut the fridge. As I crossed to the toaster, I noticed the local newspaper on one of the kitchen chairs. It was open to the business section, which my father reads religiously.

"Dad," I said, "have you ever heard of a guy named Stuart Afton?"

"You mean the cement-and-gravel tycoon?" Dad asked.

"He's a tycoon?"

Dad paused. "Maybe not exactly. But he is a big player in

the local building supplies industry. I've heard he's kind of ruthless, like a strong-arm guy."

"Hmmm." I had to admit that Afton didn't sound like the kind of person to forgive a debt. No, I told myself, rummaging for syrup, people can surprise you. Maybe Afton is tough on the outside but a softie on the inside. I pushed aside the thought that came after that: that David could also surprise me and that Hunter could be right.

Get your mind off it, I ordered myself. "Where are Mom and Mary K.?" I asked Dad.

"They went to church early to help with the Christmas clothing drive." He wiped his hand on a dish towel. "We're meeting them there for mass."

I brought my waffle over to the table and fiddled with my fork. "Um, I have a lot of studying to do," I said at last. "Is it all right if I skip church?"

Behind his tortoiseshell glasses, Dad's eyes were troubled. "I suppose so," he said after a moment.

"Thanks." I put a big bite of waffle into my mouth so I didn't have to say anything else. Since discovering Wicca, my relationship to Catholicism was changing, like everything else in my life. Though I still found the services beautiful, they didn't speak to me in the way they once had. I was pleased, though, that my parents were at a point where they accepted my ambivalence, despite the worry it caused them.

I spent most of the rest of the day tucked away in my room, studying the books Hunter had lent me. I copied spells and lessons into my Book of Shadows and even, feeling a little silly, made myself a set of rune flash cards. I wasn't going to leave Hunter any room to reprimand me for being lax in my studies.

As if he'd heard me thinking, Hunter called to suggest that I come over Tuesday afternoon for some more lessons. I couldn't think of a legitimate excuse, so I agreed.

That night I had trouble sleeping again. I was troubled by Hunter's suggestion that dark magick had anything to do with Stuart Afton's change of heart regarding Practical Magick. I couldn't believe that David would be involved in anything like that. How would I know for sure? It wasn't as if I could just go up to him and ask him.

I could scry, I realized. Maybe I'd find the proof I needed for Hunter to back off on this crazy idea. I hated that he could make me suspicious of my friends.

I peered out into the hallway. The light in my parents' room was out and so was Mary K.'s. Quietly I took the candle from the altar in my closet, set it on my desk, and lit it.

I stared into the flame, burning bright yellow with streaks of orange and blue. It seemed so insignificant. One breath could annihilate it. When I'd scryed before, I'd done it with a full, blazing fire, but in theory there was no reason why a candle shouldn't work just as well. Fire was fire, wasn't it? And right now the thought of any fire greater than this one made me shudder.

I closed my eyes and began to clear my mind. Breathe in, breathe out. In, out. I was aware of my pulse slowing, my muscles relaxing, the tiny fibers smoothing themselves into shining ribbons.

Fire, help me to see the truth. I am ready to see what you know, I thought, and opened my eyes.

The small flame of the candle had blazed up into a molten, white-hot teardrop. From its brilliant center, a face gazed back at me: a familiar nose and mouth, smooth skin, dark, thick hair, and golden eyes. That isn't David, I thought stupidly.

I stared, frozen, as Cal's image floated before me. His lips moved, and then I heard his voice.

"Morgan, I'm sorry. I love you. I'll love you forever. We're soul mates."

"No," I breathed, feeling my heart implode. It wasn't true. We weren't destined to be together. I knew that now.

"Morgan, forgive me. I love you. Please, Morgan . . ."

The last word was a whisper, and I struck out blindly with my hand and brought it down on the candle flame. There was a hiss and a faint, charring smell. And I was alone in the darkness.

12
Ugly

July, 1991

I thought Fiona was delirious from the fever, but her terror was so intense that I ended up bundling her up and putting her into Leandre's car. I chose a direction at random: east. We had driven for less than an hour when Fiona let out a cry. "Leandre!" She grasped my arm. "I can _feel_ him. He's dying."

I pulled up at the first little village bistro I could find and rushed in to phone Leandre, but I couldn't get through. Not until late that night did we find out that his farm had been consumed by a mysterious wildfire. He and all his family had been trapped in their house.

"It was the dark wave," Fiona whispered, shuddering. "It's hunting for us."

Without discussing it, we got back into the car and continued east, fleeing across France. As I drove through the *clear summer night. I kept remembering something Selene had said shortly before I left her the first time. She'd come back from a meeting with her Woodbane friends, the ones I feared, and once again she'd been in an oddly frenetic state, as if she had so much energy within her that she must keep moving or catch fire. I asked her what they'd done. "Watched the wave," she said with a strange, sharp laugh. Of course, I though she meant waves: we lived on the Pacific coast. But now, as I drove, I wondered if she'd meant something else altogether.*

Did Selene have something to do with sending the dark wave? Is she taking her revenge at last?

—Maghach

I don't know how long I sat there, shaking, too shocked even to cry. Goddess, help me, I thought desperately.

Cal. Oh, Cal. Tears began to rain down my cheeks, scalding and salty. I wrapped my arms around myself and rocked back and forth, keening quietly, trying to smother the sound. My palm throbbed where I'd crushed the candle flame, and as I sat there, the pain seemed to spread until my whole body was one pulsing, raw wound.

After a while Dagda mewed and tapped me tentatively with one paw. I looked at him numbly.

At some point my brain began to work again. How had that happened? How had Cal gotten into my vision? Was it his dark magick? Or had I summoned him somehow—had my own subconscious betrayed me?

He'd said he still loved me. He'd said he'd love me forever. Wasn't that truth I'd heard in his voice?

I gasped and squeezed my head between my hands. "Stop it. Stop it!" I muttered.

I sat there for another few minutes. Then I forced myself to climb into bed. Dagda sprang up and curled himself into a ball on my stomach. I lay there, staring blindly at the ceiling as tears ran down the sides of my face to soak my pillow.

I went through school the next day like an automaton. The burn on my palm had swelled into a shiny blister that burst halfway through the day. It hurt to write, so I just sat in class, not bothering to take notes. Not that my notes would have been much good, anyway. For all I got, my teachers might as well have been speaking Swahili. All I could think was: Cal. He had spoken to me.

What did it mean? Did he still hope to convince me to join him and Selene? Or was this some cruel plan to make me go crazy? If that was it, it was working. I'd never experienced such a horrible mixture of longing and revulsion. I felt like I was going to split apart.

When I got home from school, I had a message from Bob Unser, saying that Das Boot's parts had come in and asking me to drop off the car tomorrow morning. I could pick it up again on Wednesday morning, he said. Perfect, I thought. I couldn't possibly go to Hunter's on Tuesday since I wouldn't have transportation. I knew I was being incredibly stupid, not telling him about seeing Cal, but I just couldn't do it. I couldn't share it, especially with him. Not yet, anyway.

I shot off an e-mail to Hunter, saying I had to cancel

tomorrow because I would be vehicularly challenged. I also told him what David had told me about how he hurt his hand.

Then I sat at the kitchen table, drumming my fingers on the Formica surface. I had to do something to distract myself. I knew Aunt Eileen and Paula were moving in all week; some manual labor would be just what the doctor ordered. So I set off for Taunton.

Taunton was a smaller town than either Widow's Vale or Red Kill. Both Widow's Vale and Red Kill had had their town centers "revitalized," but Taunton was more mainstream America. There were the usual strip malls with the predictable fast-food joints, auto supply places, megastores, and video and drugstore chains.

Eileen and Paula's neighborhood was older. Although each house was different, they fit together harmoniously. Huge old trees shaded the lawns and arched out over the center of the street. The neighborhood had a nice, settled feel to it.

Paula and Eileen's house was at the very end of the street. I wanted to surprise them, so I parked at the other end of the block. I started walking.

As I got closer to the end of the block, I saw three teenage boys standing in front of one of the houses. Two of them wore parkas with shiny reflective tape on the seams. The third wore a loose camouflage jacket over camouflage pants. At first I thought they were having a snowball fight with some other kids I couldn't see; then I realized that they were throwing *rocks* at Paula and Eileen's house. My mouth dropped open, and I froze in my tracks.

"Queer!" one of them shouted.

"We don't need dykes in this neighborhood!" called another.

In one instant I got it, and then I was running hard toward the house, anger coursing through my veins like alcohol.

"Come on out, bitch!" one of the boys yelled. "Meet your neighbors! We're the welcome wagon!"

I heard the sound of glass shattering as at least one of the rocks connected. The boy closest to me looked up, his alarm quickly replaced by naked aggression.

"What the hell are you doing?" I demanded, breathing hard. "Get out of here, and don't come back!"

The boy couldn't be older than me, I saw. He had a shaved head, a nose that was nearly flat, and pale blue eyes. "Who are you?" He sounded amused. "One of their dyke friends? You don't know what you're missing, baby."

"Get. Out. Of. Here," I said, my voice vibrating with only marginally controlled fury. I felt on fire with rage.

The guy with the shaved head advanced on me, and his two friends closed in behind him. "Or what?" he said nastily. "You'll hit me with your purse?" He turned around to his friends, and the three of them laughed. My hands were trembling, clenched into fists, and I felt almost ill.

"Leave," I said, eerily calm. My voice didn't sound like my own. "Don't make me hurt you."

He burst into laughter. "Baby, maybe what you need is a man. Like those other dykes." He opened his arms wide. "Let me show you how it's supposed to be."

One of his friends laughed.

"You don't know what you're doing," I almost whispered.

Grinning, Flat Nose reached out to grab my arm, but before he touched me, I shot out my hand and sent a burning, crackling ball of blue witch fire at his throat. I didn't even think about it—I just unleashed my fury. The fire hit him so quickly, he had no time to react. His hands went to his throat, and he dropped to his knees. He doubled over, making little whimpering sounds of pain.

I felt encased in ice, completely calm, ready to annihilate them all. I began to call on my power. "An di allaigh, re nith la," I murmured.

The two friends were staring at Flat Nose and then back at me as they tried to figure out what happened. Flat Nose was gagging and retching on the cold sidewalk. He glared up at me and tried to climb to his feet. I pushed the air and he sank, crumpled, to the cement. I used my power to pin him like a bug without even touching him. Adrenaline coursed through my veins, and I felt unbelievably powerful.

"Shit," said the second guy. He and the third guy stared fearfully at each other. Then they turned and pounded down the street, looking back over their shoulders.

I leaned over the worm who lay writhing and frightened on the sidewalk. He was getting just what he deserved, I gloated with satisfaction. I felt filled with power, and I liked it.

I took a deep breath and stepped back, smelling the acrid scent of his fear. "Go," I whispered, and released him with my mind.

Clumsily he scrambled to his feet and backed away from me. Then he spun around and ran off. It was over, and I had won.

I felt dizzy, a little nauseous, the way I sometimes felt in circles when power rushed through me. I took a few moments to ground myself, then I looked up at the house.

The bay window was smashed, as well as another one on the first floor. Where were Eileen and Paula? I wondered. Were they hurt? Or had they seen what I'd done?

Wondering how I would explain it, I walked up to the door and rang the bell. Winter-bare rosebushes in front of the house were sparkling with shards of glass.

No one answered. I cast my senses and felt both Eileen's and Paula's familiar energy inside the house. They were okay. They were just afraid to answer the door, and I felt angry all over again. Prisoners in their own house. It was disgusting!

"Aunt Eileen, it's me, Morgan!" I called through the broken window.

"Morgan?" A minute later the door opened, and my aunt swept me into her arms. "Are you okay? There were these idiot boys outside—"

She hadn't seen me. Relief.

"I saw them," I told her.

Paula gave me a hug, too. "Welcome to the neighborhood," she said shakily.

We all stepped in, and Aunt Eileen shut the front door, locking the dead bolt. She crossed her arms over her chest, rubbing her own shoulders as if for comfort. "I'm glad they left before you got here," she said. "But I'm sorry they didn't stick around long enough for the police to show up. I just called them."

"We probably shouldn't clean up the glass until the police have seen it." Paula ran a hand through her sandy blond hair. "I guess we're an official crime scene now."

I felt so sorry for them—and so furious at those small-minded idiots.

"It's just glass," Aunt Eileen said, putting an arm around her. "We can have new glass put in." She looked at me. "I'm sorry, Morgan. This isn't a good welcome for you. Come in, take off your coat, and we'll give you the grand tour of broken glass and packed boxes."

We walked through the empty rooms, and Paula and Aunt Eileen explained their plans for decorating and renovating to me. They were both doing their best to sound excited, but I could sense their tension. The thugs had shaken them badly.

When the doorbell rang, we all jumped. My senses told me it was safe, though, and when Aunt Eileen opened the door, we saw two cops. Officer Jordan was a tall man and black. His partner was a younger woman with short, curly blond hair, whose badge said Officer Klein. I stood by as Aunt Eileen and Paula gave their report and showed them the damage.

"Did you get a good look at these boys?" Officer Jordan asked.

"We know there were three of them," Aunt Eileen told him. "But we stayed in the house."

"I saw them as I came up," I said. "They were about my age, juniors or seniors in high school. One of them was wearing camouflage. Another was bald with a flat, broken nose and blue eyes."

Paula looked at me in surprise. "How did you get such a good look at them?"

"They, um, they ran right past me," I explained. "Another

guy was little, maybe five-five, with a brown crew cut. The third guy had blond hair, slicked back, and thick lips."

Officer Jordan took notes on all of that, then looked at my aunt. "It looks like you people just moved in. Any idea of why these kids went after you?"

"Because we're gay," Aunt Eileen said matter-of-factly. "They called us dykes."

I noticed Officer Klein's lips tighten. "Some people are just ignorant," she muttered.

"I hope you catch them," Paula said. "Before they actually hurt someone."

The police left, and I helped Aunt Eileen and Paula clean up the shattered glass and seal off the broken windows with cardboard and tape.

"God, that's ugly," Paula said, looking at our handiwork.

"It's temporary," Aunt Eileen assured her. "I'll call a glass company tomorrow."

I glanced at my watch. "Oh, wow, I'd better get home. It's after six."

Aunt Eileen and Paula both hugged me and told me to come back anytime.

As I walked down the front steps, I turned back to wave and saw the two of them hugging each other tightly. Paula's face was buried in Aunt Eileen's shoulder. I could feel their tension from where I stood. And I knew what they were worried about. I'd had the same thought.

This wasn't over. Those kids would talk themselves out of their fear at what I'd done. And then they'd be back.

13.
Protection

Litha, 1993

We're in Prague now, but Fiona feels we'll have to leave again soon. A dubious legacy of the dark wave—ever since she saw it in her leug, she can sense it coming.

It's been two years now since we left our lives behind us. Two years of running, hiding, locking our magick away to keep it from betraying us. Two years of longing for news of our children, yet not daring to reach out to them. Two years of Fiona gradually withering, racked by ailment after ailment. We've come to believe it's the effect of the dark wave itself—that it crippled her somehow when she saw it in her leug. So far we've found no cure.

—Maghach

That night I blew off my homework. I went through every magick book I had, looking for something that would help me protect Aunt Eileen and Paula. I could put runes of protection around their house, I reasoned. That would be a start, at least.

Too bad I couldn't get them to wear talismans for personal safety. Somehow I couldn't picture either of them wearing Wicca paraphernalia, no matter how open-minded they might be.

"Ew," I said as I found the instructions for making an old protection called a Witch's Bottle. The Witch's Bottle was not only supposed to shield you from evil but also to send the evil back to its source. It called for filling a small glass bottle halfway to the top with sharp objects: old nails, pins, razor blades, needles, and so on. Then you filled the bottle the rest of the way with urine and, ideally, some blood, too. Then you sealed the jar and buried it twelve inches deep. The bottle and its protection was supposed to last until the bottle was dug up and smashed.

I put down the book, completely grossed out. Did I have the stomach to be a witch? This was disgusting. But if it would really protect Eileen and Paula . . . I read it through again. No, it wouldn't work. The Witch's Bottle was to protect against negative *magick*. The guys who'd attacked Aunt Eileen and Paula's house were negative, all right, but they weren't using magick.

I finally settled on a protection charm that I could place in their house without their noticing. It called for ingredients that I didn't have, and I decided to make a trip to Practical Magick as soon as I had my car back.

Robbie followed me and Mary K. out to Unser's on Tuesday morning, then drove us to school. My plan was to go to my mom's office after school and spend some time inputting listings, then get a ride home with her. Mary K. was going to Jaycee's house. Jaycee's mom would drop her at our house in time for dinner.

After school I set out alone on the long walk to Mom's office, shivering and hoping someone I knew would drive by and offer me a ride.

Be careful what you wish for. A familiar pale green Ford pulled up at the curb, and the passenger window rolled down. Sky Eventide leaned over from the driver's seat, her white-blond hair luminous. "Hop in," she said.

"Were you out looking for me?" I asked, perplexed. "Or is this just a coincidence?"

Sky raised an eyebrow. "Haven't you yet learned that there are no coincidences?"

I stood on the sidewalk, staring stupidly at her. Was she joking or not? I wasn't sure. Just like Hunter, Sky wasn't easy to read.

Seeing my confusion, she said, "Hunter asked me to come pick you up. I even left work early. You're supposed to come to our house for lessons."

I had heard that Sky worked at a used-record store. She was so ethereal, it was hard to picture her doing mundane things like working a cash register. "But I already told Hunter I couldn't come," I protested. "And my mom's expecting me."

Sky tapped a gloved finger on the steering wheel impatiently. "Call her from our place. This is important, Morgan."

She was right, I realized, though not for the reasons she thought. I couldn't keep putting off talking to Hunter. Biting my lip, I opened the passenger door and climbed in.

My stomach felt fluttery. I still didn't feel ready to talk about seeing Cal, but I knew I had to face it sooner or later. And sooner was probably safer.

Sky pulled out into traffic and accelerated. She drove fast and tended to stomp on the brakes harder than she needed to at red lights. "Sorry," she said as I jerked forward against my seat belt. "I'm not used to all this power-assisted driving."

I glanced at her as she made a right turn. Her profile was pure, almost childlike, with its perfect nose and arched brows, the smooth curve of cheek covered with the finest, faintest golden down. She and Hunter looked very much alike, but while Sky seemed deceptively fragile, Hunter's face had a masculine angularity that projected strength.

"Why is Hunter doing this?" I found myself asking. "Why is he so concerned about making sure that I become a proper witch?"

Sky smiled slightly. "Wicca isn't something you can learn in a correspondence course or figure out on your own. It's experiential. You need someone who's gone through it before you as a guide. Otherwise bad things can happen. Especially with the kind of power that you've inherited."

"That's not what I was asking," I said. "Why Hunter? Doesn't he have more important things to do than worry about me?"

"He's a Seeker," Sky replied. "It's his job to make sure witches don't misuse their magick. And—" She broke off. Then, after a moment's hesitation, she added, "And you're Woodbane."

I bristled. "So he's waiting for me to turn bad?"

"You might," Sky said bluntly. "He can't ignore the possibility."

I folded my arms and pressed my back against the cushioned seat. So Hunter was acting as my watchdog, making sure I stayed on the path of righteousness. I was his assignment, just as I had been Cal's assignment.

I remembered how much I had hated both Sky and Hunter when I'd first met them. With Sky it was mostly from jealousy—her beauty and poise were intimidating to me. But, I realized now, it was also that I'd sensed their suspicion. I could feel that Sky still didn't truly trust me; even though we'd scryed together, she continued to scrutinize me. Apparently Hunter was doing the same thing. The thought sent a sharp pain through me.

Hunter looked up when I walked in with Sky. "Thanks," he said to her.

"Ta," Sky said. She tossed her leather jacket on the sofa, then pointed to the phone. "Feel free," she said, then disappeared up the stairs.

"How long can you stay?" Hunter asked me. "We've got a lot to talk about."

"I'm not staying," I said. "Sorry Sky went to all that trouble, but I have work to do." I crossed to his phone. "If you won't drive me, I'll call a taxi."

Hunter rubbed a hand across his chin. "What is the matter with you?" he asked mildly.

"I don't appreciate you sending your cousin to practically kidnap me off the street," I snapped. "I told you I didn't have a ride, so I couldn't make it."

"I'm sorry." To my astonishment, he actually sounded abashed. "I—well, I thought I was doing you a favor."

"No, you didn't," I retorted. "You just wanted me to stick to your plan. What gives you the right to just waltz in out of nowhere and take charge? You think just because the International Council of Witches told you to keep an eye on me that gives you the right to run my life?"

"They—" Hunter began, but I cut him off.

"You know what? I'm really sick of being somebody's assignment." Tears filled my eyes. I blinked furiously, trying to keep them from falling. "No one seems to care about who I really am, or what I want! What about *me* in all of this?"

"Morgan—" Hunter began, but I cut him off again.

"No!" I cried. "Don't! It's my turn." My fingers curled into fists, and I felt pressure build in my chest. "You're so self-righteous about your mission and the council and all that crap, but really you want exactly the same thing as Cal and Selene did—to control me. To use me for your own purposes." To my humiliation, my voice broke. I turned my back on Hunter and stood there, biting down hard on my lower lip as I struggled to hold myself together.

He didn't say anything at first, and silence stretched between us. At last he spoke in a curiously subdued voice.

"You're not my assignment. The council didn't tell me to keep an eye on you, actually," he said.

I fought to regain my normal pattern of breathing so that I would be able to understand what he was telling me. I wanted so much to understand, to be wrong.

I heard Hunter take a deep breath, too. "I'm here of my own choice, Morgan. I did contact them about you, that's true. I told them you were a witch of exceptional power and that I wanted to see if I could help guide you. They said I could do that as long as it didn't interfere with my primary work as a Seeker—which is to track down Cal and Selene and others like them."

He paused, and I heard him take a step toward me. Then I felt a featherlight touch on my shoulder. "I don't want to control you, Morgan," he said. "That's the last thing I want."

His hand left my shoulder, his fingers lightly stroking my long hair. He was just inches behind me; I could feel the warmth of his body, and I held my breath.

"What I'm trying to do," he went on softly, "in my own clumsy way, is to give you the tools you need to understand the forces that you will inevitably come up against."

I turned to face him, searching his eyes, wondering what it was that he wanted, what I wanted. His eyes are so green, I found myself thinking, so gentle. I could feel his breath on my cheek, warm everywhere except on the wet trail of tears.

"I just want . . . ," he whispered, and trailed off.

We stood there, our gazes locked, and it seemed to me that once again the universe suspended its motion around us and the only warm, living things in it were the two of us.

Then Sky's voice called down from upstairs, "Hunter, did you remember to get cheese and biscuits?" and suddenly everything started moving again, and I stepped backward until the backs of my knees hit the worn ottoman and I sat down. I was trembling, and I found I couldn't look at Hunter.

"Um—yes, I got them," Hunter replied, his voice raspy and a little breathless.

"Right, then. I'm going to make a cheese-and-tomato

omelette. I'm starved." I heard Sky's boots clattering down the stairs. "Want some?"

"Sounds great," Hunter said. "Morgan, how about you?"

"Um—no thanks, my family will be expecting me for dinner at six-thirty," I said shakily. "In fact, I'd better give my mom a call right now and let her know where I am."

"Tell her I'll run you home by six," he said. Then he added, "If that's all right with you, I mean. If you want to stay."

"It's all right," I told him. I didn't feel ready to leave.

By the time I hung up, I felt more normal. Hunter led me to the back of the house, where the wood-burning stove filled the long room with warmth. The windows were fogged with condensation, but I rubbed one with my sweater and looked outside. Another rickety porch lined the back of the house, and beyond it I could see trees growing from the sides of the ravine: oak, maple, birch, hemlock, and pine. The woods around Widow's Vale tended to have a well-trod, gentle feel to them. But the land behind Hunter and Sky's house felt raw, wild, as though floodwaters had just swept through and carved out something new and highly charged.

"It feels different here," I said.

"It is. It's a place of power." Hunter lit the candle and incense stick on the altar. He gestured to the floor where we'd held the circle. A worn oriental carpet now covered the center of the floor. "Have a seat."

I settled myself on the carpet.

He didn't sit. "There's something we need to discuss," he said.

"What?" I asked, feeling wary again.

"I did some checking on David's story, yesterday and today.

That's why I couldn't come pick you up myself." Hunter paced toward the woodstove, then swung around to face me. "First of all, he lied about how he hurt his hand. I asked Alyce, and she told me he'd come in with it bandaged up two days *before* the party. He didn't do it trimming boughs for the party."

My heart lurched. David had lied to me?

Wait. I thought back. Not so fast. He never said he cut his hand trimming boughs *for the party*. He could have been trimming some other boughs. Couldn't he?

"Second, Stuart Afton didn't make any money on stocks last week," Hunter said.

I frowned. "I'm not following you."

Hunter made an impatient gesture with his hand. "David said Afton forgave his debt because he'd made a killing on the stock market last week," he reminded me. "But I checked, and it never happened."

"You checked? How?"

"If you must know," Hunter said, looking uncharacteristically self-conscious, "I chatted up his secretary. No man has secrets from his secretary. She knew nothing about any sudden windfall."

"And why is this your business?"

"Because I'm a Seeker," Hunter said. "It's my job to investigate misuses of magick."

"This doesn't have anything to do with magick," I said, standing up. "Maybe there was a stock split and Afton's secretary was at lunch when the call came in. Maybe he got the news by e-mail. Maybe there was no stock split but Afton forgave the debt anyway, out of the simple goodness of his heart. This isn't council business, Hunter."

"Open your eyes, " Hunter said flatly. "There's magick involved here. Dark magick. We both know that."

I realized I had no choice. I had to tell him about seeing Cal.

I took a deep breath. "There's something I have to tell you."

I explained how I'd scryed for the truth two nights ago and how instead of seeing David, Cal had appeared. I didn't speak about the feelings seeing Cal's face had induced, nor did Hunter ask. But two white creases appeared on the outsides of his nostrils.

"The way I see it, this is the strongest proof we've had yet that Cal is behind the dark magick we've detected," I said. "It isn't David at all."

I could see Hunter weighing this new information. "You say you asked to see the truth?" he asked after a moment. "Were those the words you used? Did you mention David's name?"

"No," I answered, puzzled. "Why?"

"You weren't very specific. And fire can be a capricious scrying tool," Hunter replied.

"Are you trying to tell me the fire lied to me?" I asked. I was starting to get angry again.

"No," Hunter said. "Fire doesn't lie. But it reveals the truths *it* wants to reveal, especially if you're not specific with your questions."

I put my head in my hands, feeling suddenly weary. "I don't get it, Hunter," I said. "I keep giving you clues that point clearly to Cal and Selene, the witches you came here to investigate—the witches you're still trying to track down. I don't want it to be them—I don't want to even think about them. But it makes total sense that they're the ones whose presence I felt. Why do you keep trying to make this about David and Practical Magick?"

Hunter was silent for a moment. At last he said, "It's a feeling I have. I've got an instinct for darkness. It's what makes me so good at my job." The words weren't a boast. His voice was quiet. For the first time I began to really wonder. Was it possible that he was right?

"Enough of this," he said with a sigh. "We're not getting anywhere, and it's nearly six. I'd better run you home."

We walked out to his car without talking. I noticed with a shock that it was the same gray rental sedan he'd had the week before. Selene had hidden it in an abandoned barn when she thought Cal and I had killed Hunter.

"I tracked it down," Hunter remarked, eerily echoing what was on my mind. We climbed into the car, and he drove me home in silence, each lost in our own thoughts. He pulled into my driveway. Then, as I reached for the door handle, he put his hand on mine. "Morgan."

A jolt of sensation ran up my arm, and I turned to face him.

"Please think about what we discussed, about David. I'm almost certain Stuart Afton didn't forgive that debt out of kindness."

"I just don't believe David would mess with dark magick," I said. As he began to reply, I cut him off. "I know, I know, you have a special sense for evil. But you're wrong this time. You have to be."

I climbed out and hurried up the walk to my house, hoping I was right.

14.
Old Wounds

Beltane, 1996

We are in Vienna, where I have found work tutoring college students in English. Evenings, Fiona and I walk along the Danube or in the Stefansplatz. She has gained some much needed weight and is looking better. The other night we even went on the Ferris wheel in the Volksprater. But the amusement park made us think of the children. Have Beck and Shelagh ever taken them to such a place?

Giomanach is now thirteen, Linden almost twelve, and Alwyn, nine. I wonder what they look like.

—Maghach

At dinner Mom reported that so far there had been no new incidents at Aunt Eileen and Paula's house. "They're hoping that those creeps saw the police show up at the house and have backed off."

"I hope so," I said. I reminded myself to get to Practical Magick for those ingredients soon.

Mom dished out some goulash and handed me the plate. "Will you be able to finish inputting our real estate listings this week?" she asked.

"I'm getting Das Boot back tomorrow afternoon," I said. "So I can stop by your office around three-thirty, after I drop Mary K. at home."

"I forgot to tell you. I'm not coming straight home tomorrow after school," said Mary K. "I'm going shopping with Olivia and Darcy."

Shopping. I wasn't ordinarily a big fan of shopping, but suddenly I felt a sharp pang of envy. How long had it been since I'd gone shopping with my friends or just hung out after school, doing nothing in particular?

Since you and Bree stopped being friends, I answered myself.

After dinner I went upstairs and tried to do my math homework, but my brain was too overloaded with thoughts of Hunter, Cal, David. I sighed. With its connection to the harmony of nature, Wicca was about balance, something I sorely needed. I had to bring balance back into my life, and the only way I could think of doing that was with a healthy dose of non-Wicca normalcy.

Surprising myself, I opened my door and padded out into the hall, where I picked up the phone. I took it back into my room and perched cross-legged on my bed.

My heart pounded as I dialed Bree's number. It had been so long since I'd done this. Would she want to talk to me?

Bree picked up on the third ring. "Hi, it's Morgan," I said quickly, before my nerve failed me.

"Hi." She sounded uneasy. "What's up?"

"Um—" I hadn't thought this through. "Not a whole lot. I just . . . you know, wanted to say hi. Catch up."

"Oh. Well, hi," she said.

Then we had one of those long, awkward silences, and I wondered if maybe it was crazy of me to have called her. Maybe she didn't want to be friends with me anymore. Maybe there was just too much water under the bridge.

I was about to mumble that I had to go when she spoke. "Morgan." She hesitated. "Some of things I did to you—I know they really hurt. I can't undo them. But I'm really sorry. I was a complete bitch."

"I—I was, too," I admitted.

Another silence. Clearly neither one of us wanted to go into the details. It was still too raw to bring all that up again.

"So," she said, "what's been happening in your life? Robbie told me—well, he told me about your being adopted. About being a blood witch."

"He did?" I tried to decide how I felt about Bree and Robbie discussing my personal life.

"Yeah. I've been wanting to talk to you about it. If you want to," she said.

"I've been wanting to talk to you about it, too," I confessed. "But when we're face-to-face. Not on the phone."

"Okay," she said. "I'd like that."

"Meanwhile Hunter's got me in a Wicca study intensive," I told her. "You know, he's taken over the leadership of Cirrus now that . . ." I trailed off. Now that Cal's gone, I thought. Quickly changing the subject, I asked, "How's Kithic? How is it having Sky lead a coven?"

"Challenging," Bree said in a thoughtful tone. "We've been doing visualization exercises. At our last circle we were outside under the moon, and Sky told us to visualize a pentagram. At first everyone was distracted by the cold and the noise of cars going by. Finally, though, we got it together. We all closed our eyes, visualizing away, and there was this moment of absolute silence, then Sky told us to open our eyes, and there was this perfect pentagram, etched in the snow. It was amazing."

"Cool," I said enviously. It sounded like her coven was really growing. I leaned back against my pillows.

Bree's voice went conspiratorial. "Sky and Raven are flirting, I think. Isn't that wild?"

"Very wild." It was so easy to fall back into gossiping with Bree again. "I never figured Raven would turn out to be gay."

"I don't think she really is. I think she just really likes Sky. It's an attraction of opposites," Bree said with a laugh. There was another pause, but this time it didn't feel awkward. It was just—natural.

"Speaking of attractions," I ventured, "how's your love life?"

"Robbie." I heard a guarded note in her voice.

"Yeah," I said, hoping I hadn't shattered our new, fragile bond.

But Bree just sighed. "Well, it's—it's kind of weird," she said slowly. "I don't know . . . we've been buddies forever, and now all of a sudden we're making out. I guess I'm just sort of taking it as it comes and seeing what happens." She gave a little laugh. "I have to say, though, we really click physically. It's very hot."

"Wow." I felt voyeuristic but also fascinated. It was strange to hear these two people I'd known since childhood talk about each other in these new, romantic terms.

"Listen, I've got to go," Bree said. "I've got a history paper due tomorrow, and I'm still on page one."

"You'll crank it out," I told her. "You always do."

"Yeah, I do, don't I," she replied. "I'll talk to you later, okay? And—Morgan?"

"What?"

"Thanks for calling," she said softly. "I know it couldn't have been easy to do."

"You're welcome," I said.

We hung up, and I replaced the phone on the hall table. I was smiling as I went back into my room, feeling happier than I had for days.

15.
Threads

Imbolc, 1997

    Imbolc is a day for light. Fiona reminds me that Imbolc means "in the belly," in the womb of the Goddess, and celebrates the seeds hidden in the earth that are just beginning to stir. Even though it's dark and cold here in Helsinki, it's a day of hope, and we must light the sacred fire.

    In England, among the Covens, there are great bonfires. Here we lit candles throughout our small rented house. Then the two of us did a quiet ceremony as we fed kindling into our woodstove.

    The cold is hard on Fiona. She is always shivering and in pain. We can't live this far north for long. Where next, I wonder?

    —Maghach

After my conversation with Bree the night before, I felt so much better able to face the next day. I knew she and I still had many, many fences to mend, but for the first time it actually seemed possible.

"You're in a good mood," Mary K. commented as we were getting ready for school. "Is that because you were talking to Hunter on the phone last night?" she added, wiggling her eyebrows at me.

She shrieked as I threw a damp dish towel at her.

"It wasn't Hunter. If you must know," I said, grabbing my backpack, "I was talking to Bree."

Mary K. beamed at me. "That's great!" She knew how much my friendship with Bree meant to me. "Maybe now things will get back to normal around here."

Robbie honked outside. He was giving us another lift to school. I'd pick up Das Boot later, and then things really *would* get back to normal!

Just as I was slipping into my coat, the phone rang. My witch senses tingled. What could Hunter want so early in the day? I picked up the phone. "Hi, Hunter."

"Good morning."

"I can't really talk," I told him. "I'm on my way to school, and Robbie and Mary K. are waiting for me."

"I'll make this quick," he said. "I just—I feel I need to prepare you. I know you're being loyal to David, and that's good. But I don't want you to be blind to dark forces just because you like him."

"I'm not," I said, stung. "Don't you think, after what Cal did to me, that I've learned my lesson? It just doesn't make sense to me, that's all. David's not like Selene or

Cal. He's not power hungry. He's not even Woodbane."

He drew a long breath. "Listen, I told you how my brother, Linden, died. How he called up a dark spirit and it overpowered him."

That wasn't the whole story, I knew. When we'd joined our minds, I had learned that Hunter had been accused of causing Linden's death and had stood trial before the International Council of Witches. He'd been found innocent, but he still carried the pain of his loss and the conviction of his own guilt.

"I remember," I said.

"What I didn't tell you is that Linden had called up dark spirits many times before," Hunter went on. "After that first time, when he did it with me—it was as if the door had been opened for him. He liked working dark magick. It spoke to him. But the first time, Morgan—the first time we did it for the purest of reasons."

"And you think David did the same thing," I said. "You think he opened the door."

"I think it's possible, yes."

Robbie honked again outside. "I have to go," I told Hunter. "They're waiting for me."

"We'll talk more later," Hunter said.

"Fine. Whatever." I hung up and stared at the phone for a minute. I remembered my own pleasure when I fought off those horrible guys at Aunt Eileen and Paula's. I had enjoyed it. Did that count as dark magick? No. Even if I had felt a rush from it, I was defending people I loved against an attack. That couldn't be bad.

As I walked out to the car, I made a decision. I was going

to prove that David was innocent. That Cal was the source of the evil energy Hunter was feeling. I'd go talk to Stuart Afton myself and get this all straightened out.

After school I called Stuart Afton's office to make an appointment. His secretary told me that he wasn't in the office.

"Is he sick?" I asked.

She hesitated. "He's . . . indisposed. He's been out since the middle of last week."

Something in her voice made me extend my witch senses. I picked up on strong confusion and unease. She didn't know what was wrong with her boss, I sensed, and that was very unusual.

It also occurred to me that I'd first sensed the dark presence in the middle of last week. Around the same time Afton had stopped coming into his office.

Coincidence, I told myself.

There are no coincidences, my inner witch voice said.

"Did Mr. Afton come into any large sums of money recently?" I asked on impulse.

"Not that I have any intention of answering a question like that—but you're the second person to ask it in the last few days," the secretary said, sounding amazed. "What is going on?"

"I'm not sure," I said. "Thanks for your help."

I hung up and looked up Afton's home address. He lived in a fancy section of town, but one I could get to by bus. I didn't want Robbie to know what I was doing. Somehow I felt I needed to do this alone. I'd just take the bus back to pick up Das Boot.

The bus let me off a few blocks from Afton's house. The

houses were enormous, with wide lawns. Even the snow looked more elegant in this neighborhood. I walked fast, trying to stay warm, my breath forming a little fog in front of me.

I rang the bell and stamped my booted feet on the welcome mat. Was I nuts coming here? Would Afton even see me? I heard footsteps on the other side of the door, and then it swung open. A thick woman in a maid's uniform looked at me. A wave of worry radiated from her.

"Yes?" she asked. "May I help you?"

"Uh," I said brilliantly. "I was wondering if I could talk to Mr. Afton?"

She pursed her lips, and I realized she looked pale. "Oh, dear, I'm sorry. Mr. Afton . . . Mr. Afton . . . was taken to the hospital earlier this morning."

"What?" I gasped.

She nodded. "The paramedics thought he'd had a stroke."

"I—I'm so sorry," I stammered. My heart thudded hard. It's just a coincidence. It has nothing to do with magick, I told myself.

A crumpled shopping bag sitting in the hallway behind her caught my eye. It seemed so out of place, just lying there, as if perhaps Mr. Afton had been holding it when he'd suffered from his stroke. The forest green color and silver handles looked familiar. I was about to ask the maid about it when my witch senses tingled. Hunter was coming up the walk.

What was he doing here? I whirled and stared at him.

"Is everything all right?" he asked as he reached the door.

"Stuart Afton is in the hospital," I blurted. "He had a stroke this morning."

Hunter's green eyes widened slightly. He glanced at the maid. "I'm sorry to hear that. Can you tell me what hospital he's in? I'd like to send over some flowers."

"Yes—Memorial. That's the closest." She shook her head. "He runs six miles a day, more on weekends. You've never met anyone who takes better care of their health than Mr. Afton. A stroke just doesn't make sense."

I didn't need to do a mind meld to know what Hunter was thinking. A stroke made sense if dark magick was involved.

"Thank you. We're sorry to have bothered you," I said to the maid. Then I grabbed Hunter's arm and pulled him down the porch steps. "What are you doing here?" I demanded.

"The same thing you are, I suppose," he replied. "Trying to get some answers."

I didn't want to think about the conclusions I knew he was jumping to.

"Where's your car?" he asked as we reached the curb.

"I have to go pick it up from the shop," I said.

"Hop in. I'll give you a lift."

I stood on the sidewalk. I wasn't sure if I wanted to get into the car with him, knowing the conversation we were about to have. My stomach felt knotted.

"Morgan, make up your mind. I'm freezing." Hunter walked around the car and slid in behind the steering wheel.

I was freezing, too. I climbed into the car and told him how to get to Unser's.

I didn't know what to think and was lost in my own thoughts while Hunter drove. True, sometimes people did have inexplicable strokes. Maybe he had some congenital defect.

"Someone like Stuart Afton is a very unusual candidate for a stroke," Hunter pointed out, and though it was exactly what I'd been thinking, I felt a flash of irritation. Hunter always had to be right.

"It happens," I said. "All kinds of freak things happen. Look at my life."

Hunter nodded. "Exactly. Your life was straight-on normal until magick kicked in. I could say the same for Afton, except magick has dealt with him far more harshly than it has with you."

"You don't know that this has anything to do with magick," I reminded him tightly. "You're jumping to conclusions."

"Am I?" he asked.

I took a deliberate breath and tried to keep my tone reasonable. "Okay, for the sake of argument, let's say David did have something to do with Afton erasing the debt. Well, Afton did it. David has the shop. So why would David hurt him now? He's grateful to Afton. Hurting him now doesn't make sense."

"Unless David made mistakes, got involved with forces he can't control, lost his power over what was supposed to happen," Hunter said. "The darkness is not predictable. It often has effects beyond the immediate, planned ones."

He sounded so self-righteous that I lost my temper and words shot out of my mouth. "You know what? I think being a Seeker makes you suspicious of everyone. I think you're furious because Cal and Selene escaped, so now you're determined to get someone else. David just happens to be a convenient target."

The brakes squealed as Hunter suddenly swerved and pulled off the road. I barely had time to brace myself before he cut off the engine and turned to face me, his eyes blazing with anger. "You have no idea what you're talking about! Do you think this a *game* for me, where I cut notches in my belt for every renegade witch I run in? Do you think I get off on going after other witches?"

My own temper caught fire. "You do it, though, don't you? You *chose* it."

The muscle in his jaw twitched, and one hand clenched the steering wheel, his knuckles white. Then Hunter relaxed suddenly, releasing the tension from his body on a deep breath. He rubbed his hand over his chin, the way he did when he was thinking. The car was filled with the vanishing traces of our anger, our quiet breathing. The air seemed alive and crackling, and it occurred to me that when I was with Hunter, I literally felt more alive. Probably because I was so often angry at him. But when I was with him, I didn't have time to be crushed with sorrow over Cal.

"Morgan, it's important to me that you understand that what you accused me of—is not true," Hunter said, his voice low. "That's not what being a Seeker is. If the council even suspected me of acting that way, they'd strip me of my powers in a heartbeat. I don't understand how you could think that of me."

His gentle answer made me ashamed. "Okay," I said. "Maybe I was wrong." I've always been a rotten apologizer. It was one of the things I wanted to work on.

"Maybe?" He shook his head and started the car again. Neither one of us spoke after that until we were almost at Unser's. We drove past the entrance to the Afton Enterprises gravel pit, and I saw him turn his head to read the sign. When he faced front again, he was frowning.

We pulled into Unser's yard. "Is this where you felt that dark energy?" Hunter asked me, his frown deepening. "Right here?"

"Yes," I said, puzzled.

"What day was it?" Hunter asked.

"Last Wednesday," I said, but then I saw Das Boot parked over to the side, and I forgot everything else. My beloved white car had a new hood and new bumper, but the hood was *blue*.

"Oh my God," I gasped. "My car!"

Bob Unser heard Hunter's car and came out of the garage, wiping his hands on a rag. Max, the German shepherd, loped out at his side, grinning amiably. Hunter and I climbed out of his car, and I walked slowly to my Valiant, feeling like I was about to cry.

Bob looked over Das Boot with pride. "Good fit, huh?" he asked. "That hood is perfect. We got lucky."

I was speechless. The two front sides of my car had been hammered out and covered with Bondo body filler to fix the crumpling. The Bondo was sanded and looked like steel-gray dusty spackle all over the front of my car. And the hood was *blue*. The bumper looked all right, but was unusually shiny and looked out of place. My beautiful, lifesaving car looked like crap.

"Uh . . . uh . . ." I began, wondering if I was going to hyperventilate. After losing my boyfriend, almost being killed, having my magick disappear on me in a circle, worrying about David Redstone; now, ridiculously, what was finally sending me over the edge was owing my parents almost a thousand dollars so my car could look like *crap*.

Hunter patted my shoulder. "It's just a car," he offered hesitantly.

I couldn't even respond. My mouth just hung open.

Bob gave me a look. "Course, it needs to be painted," he said.

"Painted?" I was amazed at how calm my voice was.

"I didn't want to do that without talking to you," he explained, scratching his head. "We can paint it white, to match the rest of the car, but to tell you the truth, the whole car needs a paint job. See those bits of rust under the door? We should really sand those out, give it a coat of rust protector, then paint the whole body. If we Bondo the other dings, this car could look brand-new." The idea seemed to fill him with enthusiasm.

"How much?" I whispered.

"Another four hundred, five hundred, max," he said.

I gulped and nodded. "Um, does it run okay?"

"Sure. I had to tighten the engine block a bit, knock a few hoses tighter. But this baby's a tank. It was mostly bodywork."

Max panted his agreement.

Silently I handed Bob Unser the check my mother had made out, and he dropped the keys into my hand. "Let me think about the paint job," I said.

"Sure thing. Take care of this car, now." He headed back into the warmth of the garage, and I turned to face Hunter. It was dark now, but I could still see Das Boot's tricolored nose, and it made me incredibly upset.

"I'm sorry about your car," Hunter said. "I'm sure it will be fine."

I closed my eyes and nodded. It was obvious he didn't understand at all.

16.
Uncertain

The witch from Boston came today. We spent the morning purifying Selene Belltower's house. But we had no luck getting into her library. In fact, this time I couldn't even find the door.

Then, in the afternoon, I fought with Morgan. I pushed her too hard about David. She's resisting me all the way. And why not, when it seems I'm doing nothing but persecute the people she cares for? Am I trying to make her hate me?

No, it's not that simple. I need her to be able to face the truth, even when it's ugly or painful. I need her to believe in her own strength, the strength that I see every time I look at her.

I've never met anyone who affects me the way she does. We argued today, and the things she said were so wrong and hurtful that I wanted to shake her. But then, later, when she saw what the mechanic had done to that old wreck of a car she drives, she looked so shattered, so utterly forlorn, that it was all I could do not to take her in my arms and kiss away the tears.

—Giomanach

In my hideous, piebald car, I drove to a fabric shop to get gold cloth and crimson embroidery thread. I needed them for the protection charm I was going to make for Aunt Eileen and Paula. It would be a little pouch embroidered with the rune Eolh, containing herbs and a crystal.

After that I drove to my mom's realty office. Das Boot no longer made a grinding metallic noise; in fact, the engine sounded perfect. But I was ashamed of how my beloved car looked. I parked at an angle and tried not to look at the nose as I walked to Mom's office.

Widow's Vale Realty was in a small, white-shingled building. Inside, the look was deliberately cozy, with polished hardwood floors, lots of plants, and arts-and-crafts-style rugs and furniture.

"Oh, Morgan, honey. Hi. Did you get your car?" My mom peered out from a desk piled high with three-ring binders, file folders, and loose computer printouts. She looked overworked and overwhelmed. I sighed. I was glad I'd be able to help.

"Yes," I said. "It's fixed. But please don't make me talk about how it looks."

My mom tried unsuccessfully to bite back a smile. A non–car lover, like Hunter. What strange creatures they were.

Thursday and Friday were uneventful days at Widow's Vale High. I met with Cirrus on Friday morning before classes. Everyone was excited about having a circle the following night with Hunter.

"I've been reading this guy, Eliade, who's an expert in the history of religions, and Eliade talks about sacred space," Ethan said. "I'm thinking that's where Hunter took us. And that's exactly what ritual is supposed to do."

I tried not to gape. If anyone had told me two months ago that Ethan Sharp would be discoursing on ritual and sacred space, I'd have told them they were nuts.

"That never happened with Cal," Jenna pointed out. "We did feel magick that one time, but with Hunter it was different. It was just this incredible . . . connection."

"That first circle with Hunter changed me," Sharon stated. "I can never go back to thinking about anything the way I did before."

Suddenly I realized they were all feeling something similar to what I'd felt during our very first circle with Cal, when he'd opened me up to magick. It *had* changed everything. And I ought to be feeling glad instead of resenting the coven and Hunter because my own experience in the circle had been so frustrating.

Matt, whom I'd considered totally self-absorbed, caught me off guard. "But Morgan didn't like it," he said. "It's funny that Hunter has all this power and the one blood witch among us doesn't think he's so great."

Blood witch? I looked up.

"Robbie told us. It sort of came out when he was explaining about Cal," Jenna said gently. "It's okay. We pretty much knew, anyway."

"Uh," I started, flustered. "It's not that I don't like Hunter."

"What is it, then?" Sharon asked.

It was complicated. It was Cal, losing Cal. Hunter being a Seeker and the one who'd made me see the truth about Cal. Hunter suspecting David of dark magick. I shook my head. I couldn't even begin to explain it. So I just shrugged and said, "I don't know, exactly."

Fortunately the first bell rang then. I hurried away, mumbling about how I had to get to my locker. How could I explain my feelings about Hunter to them when I couldn't even explain them to myself?

Saturday dawned cold and bleak. I woke up just after sunrise—unusual for me—shaken by a dream I couldn't remember. Dagda was curled up against my chest. I kissed the top of his silky head and tried to fall back asleep, but it was useless. My thoughts were already roiling. Hunter's face kept rising in front of my eyes. I wondered how Stuart Afton was doing. I needed to get a start on my physics homework and also get back to the realty office to input listings.

That night I had a circle, and Hunter wanted to get together on Sunday for a lesson. I'd told Aunt Eileen and Paula that I'd help them unpack sometime during the weekend, but what I really needed to do was get the last ingredients for my protection charm so I could place it in their house. That meant I had to go to Practical Magick and face David. Would he be able to sense my uncertainty about him?

Already totally stressed, I gave up on sleep, got out of bed, and got dressed. Then I settled at my desk and opened my physics book. *Plot the trajectory of a baseball that's been struck by a batter at a 45-degree angle and is traveling at 100* mph (assuming no air resistance), read the first problem. "Why?" I muttered. It was hard to imagine anything more irrelevant to my life, but I started crunching numbers and kept at it until nine, which seemed a respectable hour for me to show up for breakfast on a Saturday morning.

My mom was already gone when I got downstairs, the weekends being prime workdays for realtors. My dad sat at the table, reading the paper. "Morning, sweetie," he said.

Mary K. was standing at the stove, stirring something in a pot. "Want some oatmeal?" she asked.

"No thanks." I started to prepare my own nutritious breakfast regimen of Pop-Tart and Diet Coke.

She scraped her oatmeal into a bowl. "I talked to Aunt Eileen last night, and I'm going over there after church tomorrow to help them unpack. Want to come?"

"Yes, I told them I would. But can we talk about it later?" I said. "I've got a million things to do this weekend, and I'm not sure how the timing's going to work out."

My father lowered the paper. "What do you have to do?"

I blew out a stream of breath as I carefully edited my answer. "Um . . . working at Mom's office, errands, schoolwork, and getting together with friends tonight." My parents knew that on Saturday nights I attended Wiccan circles, but I tried not to mention it directly too often.

My father studied me with concern. "I trust schoolwork isn't coming last on your list?"

"No," I assured him. "I already did my physics. I've still got a history paper to work on, though."

He smiled at me. "I know you've got a lot going on. I'm proud of you for keeping your grades up, too."

Just barely, I thought.

Twenty minutes later I was out the door.

The light scent of jasmine was in the air when I entered Practical Magick, and Alyce was dressed in an ivory knit dress with a pale pink tunic over it. A strand of rose quartz beads hung from her neck.

"You look ready for spring." I said. "Three months early."

"There's nothing wrong with wishful thinking," she told me with a smile. "How are you, Morgan?"

"Overwhelmed but okay." I couldn't help asking, "Did you hear about what happened to Stuart Afton?"

"Yes, poor man. It's awful." She shook her head, her blue eyes troubled. "I thought maybe we would try to send him healing energy at our next circle."

"So . . . how is your coven going?" I knew that Alyce had been asked to lead Starlocket now that Selene was gone.

Alyce tucked a strand of gray hair back into its twist. "Selene is a hard act to follow. I don't have nearly the power she had. Then again, I've never abused my power the way she did. Our coven has a great deal of healing to do, and since I've always loved healing work, that will be my focus, at least for the present."

"Morgan, good morning," David said, emerging from behind a bookshelf. I noticed his hand was still bandaged and that some blood had seeped through it, staining the gauze. "Nice to see you."

I hoped my voice sounded natural as I said, "You too. Um, I need some ingredients." I took my list out of my pocket.

If he noticed anything in my manner, he didn't mention it. He simply took the list and scanned it. "Oils of cajeput, pennyroyal, lavender, and rose geranium," he murmured, nodding. "We've just gotten in a fresh stock of pennyroyal, haven't we, Alyce?"

"Yes. I'll get the oils," Alyce said. To me she explained, "We keep the big bottles in the back, by the sink. They're rather messy to handle. I'll be back in a few minutes."

She bustled off, leaving me alone with David. He looked up from my list. "Burdock, frankincense, and a sprig of ash," he said in a neutral voice.

"Do you have them?" I asked. I couldn't read him at all, and it was making me nervous.

"We've got them," he replied. He added in a conversational tone, "These are the ingredients for a protection charm. So what are you protecting yourself against?"

"It's not for me," I told him. "It's for my aunt and her girlfriend. They just moved into a house in Taunton, and they're being harassed because they're gay."

"That's a shame. It's never easy to be different," David said thoughtfully. "But I guess you know that, being a witch."

"Yes," I agreed. "Do you think this charm will really help?"

"It's worth trying."

"I used my power to stop the guys who were scaring them," I admitted. "With witch fire." I wanted to see how he would react to this turn in the conversation.

David raised one silver eyebrow but said nothing.

"Even now I want to see them suffer. It makes me worry about myself," I added.

David pursed his lips. "You're being very hard on yourself.

You're a witch, but you're human, too, with human weaknesses. Anyway, dark energy is not in and of itself necessarily evil." He slid his hand into the display case beneath the counter and took out a necklace with the yin-yang circle worked in white and black onyx. "To me, the most interesting part of this symbol is that the white half contains a tiny spot of black and the black a tiny spot of white," he said. "You need both halves—bright and dark—to complete the circle. They're part of a whole, and each contains the seed of the other. So there's no such thing as dark magick without a bit of light in it or bright magick without a bit of dark."

Alyce, who'd returned with some vials of oil while he was speaking, shook her head. "That's fine as philosophy, David, but on a purely practical level, I think we'd all do well to shun the dark."

David smiled at me. "There you have it, the combined wisdom of Practical Magick. Make of it what you will."

A customer came in, and Alyce went over to help her.

David rang up my items. Then he reached down and pulled up a paper shopping bag and put it on the counter. He set the vials inside it. "Like it?" he asked, seeing my eyes on the bag. "We had them made as part of our celebration of Practical Magick's new lease on life, as it were."

"It's nice," I managed. Grabbing the bag, I mumbled a good-bye and hurried out of the store.

Outside, I held up the bag and stared at it. It was forest green, with silver handles. Just like the bag I had seen lying crumpled in Stuart Afton's hallway the day he'd had a stroke.

17.
Breaking In

August, 1999

Beck contacted us today. I knew as soon as I saw his face in my leug that the news was bad. But I didn't imagine it would be this bad.

Linden was killed, Beck told us, trying to summon the dark spirits. "He called on the dark side to ask how to reach you and Fiona," was what Beck said in his blunt way.

Goddess, what have I wrought? I've abandoned four children, and now one is dead because of me. I didn't know this kind of pain was possible.

—Maghach

I sat in Das Boot, trying to take meditative breaths to calm down. It doesn't mean anything, I told myself. It's just a shopping bag.

Right. Afton was just the type to shop at Practical Magick.

Twenty minutes later I pulled up in front of Afton's sprawling home. What was I doing here? How was I going to prove anything?

I gazed gloomily out my car window. It must be garbage day, I realized, spotting the cans lining the curbs.

Could my proof be in those cans? I wondered. I scrambled out of the car and raced to the cans in front of Afton's house. I opened one, and the stink hit me. Ew. Was I really going to paw through someone else's trash?

I held a hand over the can, trying to get a sense of what I was looking for. I seek witch power, I thought. If there is an object that has been handled by a witch, lead me to it, please. The tips of my fingers tingled, and I ripped open one of the black plastic bags.

A green shopping bag with silver handles lay on top. The logo for Practical Magick was stamped on its side in silver. A gift card was tied to one of the handles. With shaking hands, I pulled it out of the garbage. I flipped open the card and gasped. *These are for you,* the card read. *You know why.*

The card was signed, *Blessed be, Alyce.*

I dropped the bag as if it had bitten me. Home-baked muffins tumbled out into the snow.

A car drove up and stopped behind me. Once again, I realized, Hunter had tracked me down.

"Morgan, what is it?" he asked.

I lifted my stricken face to him. "It can't be," I whispered.

If Alyce had used dark magick to cause Stuart Afton's stroke, then everything that I thought I knew or understood was wrong. And no one was to be trusted.

"Get in the car," Hunter ordered.

I simply obeyed. My mind whirled. Alyce? Then she was an amazing liar because she had seemed to be very certain that no one should mess with dark forces.

Hunter got out of the car and picked up the bag I had dropped. He gathered up the muffins, sniffed them, gazed at them. Then he dumped everything back into the garbage can. He climbed back into the car.

"They're not spelled," he said.

"Wh-what?" I asked.

"The muffins, the bag, the note," he explained. "None of it is spelled. Alyce had nothing to do with Afton's stroke."

I leaned back and let out a sigh of relief.

I felt Hunter's eyes on me. "You suspected David, though, didn't you? That's why you came back out here?"

"I—I don't know what I thought," I said.

"I went to Red Kill, to Memorial Hospital. I saw Stuart Afton," Hunter said.

I didn't bother to ask how he had been able to see Afton since he wasn't a relative or even a friend.

"I had heard he'd been acting strangely for days, which they believe may have been signaling the stroke, despite the fact that there was no medical reason for it to have happened. And he was sort of babbling while I was there."

"What did he say?" I asked apprehensively.

"He said, 'I did what they wanted. Why isn't it over?'"

"That doesn't mean anything," I felt compelled to say. "He could have been talking about work or something."

"There's more," Hunter said. "Remember the dark presence you felt at your garage? I hadn't realized until I drove you there that the garage is right down the road from the Afton gravel pit. But when I saw that, I realized that the dark presence might not have been looking for you at all."

I gaped at him. "You mean . . . ?"

Hunter nodded. "Maybe it was looking for Stuart Afton."

I put a hand to my forehead. I didn't know whether to be relieved or upset. If the dark presence had been after Afton instead of me, that meant I wasn't being stalked. But it also meant that Hunter was right and David had called on the dark side.

"Anyway, I was heading over to his office to do some more checking, then I got this sense that you needed me," Hunter said.

I bristled. "I was fine," I said. "It was just upsetting to think that Alyce might have been involved somehow."

"Well . . . good," Hunter said. "So I'll see you later."

I turned in my seat to face him. "I'm going with you."

"What?"

"I am part of this now," I said firmly. "If you're going to check out Afton's office, then I'm going, too."

For a moment it seemed like he was going to argue with me, but then he sighed. "Fine. You'd just follow me, anyway."

I managed a grin. "Gee. I guess you do know me after all."

I scrambled out of his car and into mine. Then I followed him to Stuart Afton Enterprises. Hunter took my arm, and we crossed the street to Afton's building. "I want to get into his office and search for signs of magick."

"You mean like breaking and entering?" My voice sounded strangled. I'd never even so much as shoplifted.

"Well, yes," Hunter said. "Not to put too fine a point on it."

"Don't tell me: You're a Seeker and have some sort of magickal permission that lets you break all kinds of human laws." I crossed my arms over my chest.

Hunter smiled, and I caught my breath at how boyish he suddenly looked. "That's right," he said. "You can back out anytime. I didn't invite you, remember?"

I rolled my eyes. "I'm in."

"Fine. Just so long as you remember who's in charge here."

I gritted my teeth in irritation as he murmured under his breath, quickly tracing runes and other sigils in the air. "This is a spell of illusion," he told me. "Anyone looking at us here will see something else—a cat, a banner, a tall plant—anything but us."

I was impressed and also envious of Hunter's ability. I realized again how much I had to learn.

"All right, now. Here's something for you to do," Hunter instructed. "There's an alarm wired into this door. It runs on electricity, which is just energy. Focus your own energy, then probe inside for the energy of the security system and do something with it."

I didn't want this responsibility. "What if I short-circuit the microwave by mistake?"

"You won't," he assured me.

I sent my energy inside the building. It was the first time I'd ever tried to focus on energy that wasn't attached to a person or somehow linked to the land. This was searching for electric currents that had no character or easily recognizable pattern; they were simply circuits, designed to register a response when they were opened or closed.

At first all I felt was a general emptiness within the rooms of the building. I probed again and this time felt a lower-level energy around the perimeter of the building, steady and unobtrusive, designed to be noticed only if it were broken. It ran across all the doors and through the glass of the windows. I went deeper into the building and picked up other kinds of energy—ultrasonic sound waves and, upstairs, a laser, both motion detectors. And something else on the ground floor: a passive infrared light, designed to pick up on the infrared energy given off by an intruder's body heat.

"Well?" Hunter asked.

"This is so cool," I murmured.

"Find the security system," he reminded me.

"Right." I cast my energy again, found the security control box in the basement, and let my mind examine it. I concentrated harder, sensing a pattern that had been punched in time and time again.

"Six-two-seven-three-zero," I said. "That's the code."

"Excellent." Hunter tapped the numbers into the keypad by the door, and we heard a quiet click. "Let's go."

Inside, Hunter headed for a big, windowed room at the back of the first floor: Stuart Afton's office. Inside the room he looked around, closed his eyes for a moment, and controlled his breathing. Then he reached into his jacket pocket and pulled out an athame. The hilt had a simple design, set with a single dark blue sapphire.

Hunter unsheathed the blade and pointed it at Afton's desk. A sigil flickered, lit with sapphire blue light. Magick had been done here.

Hunter pointed the blade at Afton's chair and I saw the rune Hagell, for disruption. The rune Neid, for constraint, flickered over the doorway. There were other signs that I didn't recognize.

"These are used to mark targets," Hunter explained, holding the athame at some of the unfamiliar figures. "Do you still doubt that magick has been used against Afton?"

"No." Seeing these sigils, knowing they had been wrought with dark intent, was deeply upsetting. "But we still don't know whose magick this is."

"Don't we?" His voice was soft, dangerous. He held the athame to the sigil once more. "From which clan do you arise?" he asked.

The shape of a crystal flickered above the sigil.

"What is that?" I asked.

"The sign of the Burnhides," Hunter said. He didn't sound triumphant, just sad.

"Oh, no," I said. I felt hollow inside.

"This isn't real proof," Hunter said. "There are probably other Burnhides in the area besides David. Making magick is like handwriting—if you know someone's work, you can recognize it. I need to learn David's magickal signature. Then I'll have the proof I need."

I swallowed. "Great."

Hunter and I split up after leaving Afton's offices. Needing a break from the strain, I went home.

I walked in to find Mary K. sitting at the kitchen table, white-faced.

"What's wrong?" I asked quickly, thinking, Bakker.

"Aunt Eileen just called."

"What happened? Are they all right?"

She nodded, looking stricken. "Nobody was hurt, but those guys—or some of their buddies—came back last night. This morning they found the front of the house covered with spray paint."

"What did it say?"

"Aunt Eileen wouldn't tell me," said Mary K. "So I guess it was bad. They just got back from the police station."

I felt a surge of irrational guilt. If I hadn't gone to Practical Magick and then been with Hunter . . .

"I've never heard Aunt Eileen sound so shaken up," Mary K. went on. "She called here looking for Mom, and I could tell she'd been crying. She wants to put the house on the market."

"What? Oh, no! She can't be serious!"

Mary K. shook her head, her perfect bell of auburn hair brushing her shoulders. "They're tired of the Northeast. They think that in California, people will be more tolerant." Her voice trembled. "Aunt Eileen wants Mom to relist their house."

"That's crazy!" I said. "It's just three high school kids! Three idiots, three losers. Every town has them."

"Tell that to Aunt Eileen and Paula," Mary K. said. She got up and began taking clean dishes out of the dishwasher. "God, they were so excited about that house. I hate it that anyone is doing this to them!"

"I do, too," I said. And I can do something about it, I thought.

I glanced at my watch. I had about four hours before I had to be at Jenna's house for our circle. That would give me time to finish the protection charm. And to find a spell to teach those thugs a lesson they'd never forget.

18.
Lost and Found

Fiona is dying.

The news of Linden's death broke her, I think. She'd been in pain before, but she had a core of toughness that kept the illness at bay. But in the last two years she has been . . . fading. Her hair, once so bright, is entirely white now, and her green eyes are sunk deep in her gaunt face. I see her agony, but I can't bear the thought of losing her, my dearest love, the only precious thing I have left.

This morning I broke the silence and sent a message to Giomanach. I didn't contact him directly, but I cast a spell that would open a door to him, that would let him know that we're alive. Now I'm living in terror that I've exposed him to the dark wave.

—Maghach

I was the first one to show up at Jenna's house. "This isn't like me," I said. "I'm never early." The truth was, I'd driven faster than I usually did. I felt weirdly edgy. Maybe because I was nervous about my decision to deliberately work a dark spell on the jerks who'd been harassing my aunt. Or maybe just because I was worried about going through another circle without connecting to my power.

Jenna took my coat. "All the others are running late. Ethan convinced them to go to a lecture at the Red Kill library with him. It's on sacred space and mythic time. I think it's being given by someone who studied shamanism."

"You didn't want to go?" I asked, following her into the Ruizes' comfortably shabby living room.

"With Matt? No thanks. I mean, I'm stuck in the same coven with him, but if I have a chance to avoid him, I take it."

"It must be awful to break up with someone after four years of being together," I said inadequately. Considering how I was pining over Cal, whom I had known barely three months, I could hardly imagine what Jenna was going through.

Jenna removed a large basset hound from the couch. "Go sleep in your own bed," she said. "We're having company." The dog padded off placidly, and Jenna turned to me. "Yeah. At first I just didn't know how to get through the days. Raven Meltzer!" She wrinkled her nose in disgust. "Of anyone he could have picked. I was so humiliated."

We sat down on the couch, and a big gray-and-white-striped cat jumped onto Jenna's lap, purring. She petted it absentmindedly. "We've been together since I was thirteen. I didn't know what to do without him. And everyone knew.

But now—" She shrugged. "It's amazing. I'm getting over it. I'm finding out that I'm different without Matt." She shook her head, and her fine, pale blond hair swished in a shining wave. "When I was with Matt, I was always checking in with him. I don't even know how I got into that habit. But there was nothing I did that Matt didn't know about."

The doorbell rang then, and I waited while Ethan, Sharon, Matt, and Robbie came into the house, all talking at once. "Sorry we're late," Robbie said, giving Jenna a casual hug. "We got hung up in traffic in Red Kill."

"Yeah, the place was packed," Matt said. "I had no idea that so many people even knew where the Red Kill library was."

I felt Hunter coming up the walk, and an unexpected sense of anticipation made me sit up straighter.

"My apologies, everyone," he said as he unzipped his jacket a minute later. He looked around, seeming pleased that everyone was there. "Since we're running late, let's get started. Jenna, what do you have for forming a circle?"

"Chalk, candles, incense, water," she answered.

"Perfect. Then if you'll get them and if everyone else will form a circle . . ."

Hunter quickly drew the circle and chanted an invocation to the Goddess and the God.

"I want to concentrate on things that have been lost," he said when we'd raised the energy of the circle. It was flowing among us so strongly that I could almost see it—a ribbon of light, linking and encompassing us in its strength. This time I felt more connected to it.

"Each of you, think of something lost that you want to be found," Hunter went on. "Don't say it aloud, but silently ask the energy of the circle to open a way inside you to find what's been lost."

What had I lost? My heart, was my immediate answer. But even to me that sounded too melodramatic to ask the energy of the circle to act on it.

My mind wandered, my connection to the circle weaker. I glanced at Hunter, wondering if he knew. His eyes were open, but whatever he was seeing wasn't in the room. He looked aeons away.

I closed my eyes, trying to find my connection again. Suddenly I was filled with a rush of emotion, a deep sense of loss, a yearning that I knew wasn't my own. I saw a man I didn't recognize, tall, with brown eyes and graying hair.

Father, something said within me. Father.

My eyes flew open. Somehow I knew I'd just seen Hunter's father. I had somehow picked up the images that he was experiencing in the circle.

Startled, Hunter's head whipped toward me. I flushed. I hadn't meant to invade his privacy in that way. I hoped he'd know that.

I felt him refocus, connecting to the rest of the group, and then he began taking the circle down. Once again we sat in a circle on the floor. Hunter avoided my eyes. He gave the others an apologetic look. "Would you please excuse us?" he asked. "Morgan, may I speak to you?"

Before I had a chance to answer, he was on his feet and steering me by my elbow to Jenna's kitchen.

"That was an abuse of power," he hissed at me. "You had no right!"

My mouth dropped open. "I didn't do it on purpose!"

Hunter's nostrils flared as he breathed in and out rapidly, trying to calm down. I couldn't tell if the two bright spots on his cheeks were anger or embarrassment.

I thought about how much I hated it when I felt he'd read my thoughts. He must feel awful, I realized. "I'm sorry. I truly, really, and totally have no idea how that happened."

He stared down at the tile floor. His breathing was returning to normal. "All right," he said shakily. "All right. I believe you."

"How could that have happened?" I asked. "I had a stray thought about you, and then I just . . . received all these images."

He nodded a few times, still not lifting his head. "We . . . we had a connection. That's all."

"That was your father, wasn't it?" I asked.

He looked at me, his green eyes glinting. "It was incredible," he half whispered. "I suddenly *knew*, clear as daylight, that I could call to my father, and he would hear me."

"You mean, you think he's alive?" Hunter's parents had disappeared when he was eight—more victims of the dark wave, the evil force that had destroyed Belwicket and other covens. Hunter, his brother, Linden, and their sister, Alwyn, had been taken in by their Uncle Beck and Aunt Shelagh. It had been hard, not knowing what had happened to his mother and father. No wonder it was what he focused on when thinking of something lost.

When Hunter looked at me, his eyes were full of pain. "Yes."

"Will you call to him?"

"I don't know. It's been so long since I've seen him—I

don't even know who I'd be calling. And I'm not sure he'd want to see what I've become."

"A Seeker?" I felt confused.

Hunter nodded. "We're not exactly popular among witches."

"You're the youngest member of the council. Wouldn't any Wiccan father be proud of that?"

"He's Woodbane," Hunter reminded me. "For all I know, he calls on the dark side, too."

"Don't you ever get tired of looking at the world that way?" I asked, feeling suddenly almost sorry for him. "This is your father! You haven't seen him in more than ten years. My God, if I could see my birth mother just once—"

"Ethan, quit it!" The sounds of Sharon's giddy laughter came through the kitchen door. Hunter gazed at it, as if he'd forgotten where we were.

"We'd better go back out there," he said.

I was reluctant to end this conversation. We were really talking to each other, not fighting, not having a lesson. But the others were waiting.

We went back into the living room, where the others instantly gathered around Hunter.

"I've been reading that book you told me about," Matt began. "And I don't get the part about the Four Watchtowers."

I watched for a few minutes as Hunter patiently answered their questions, in spite of all I knew he was feeling. His breadth of knowledge was impressive, and I knew he had much to teach me, including his ability to reach out to others and help them learn, even when he must be feeling so distressed.

Then it was time to leave. I got into Das Boot and sat for

a few moments, letting the engine warm up. Christmas lights were already twinkling from most of the houses on Jenna's street. The house directly across from hers had a giant illuminated sleigh and reindeer spanning the width of the roof. I have got to start getting ready for Christmas, I reminded myself, resolving to talk to Mary K. tomorrow about possible gift ideas.

Das Boot was ready to roll, so I shifted into gear. Then I shifted back into park. I couldn't just drive off, I realized, not after Hunter had revealed himself to me that way. He'd been seriously shaken, and I didn't want to just leave him.

Shifting back into drive, I drove around the block so that the others wouldn't see me. I felt very protective of the conversation I was going to have with Hunter. It was private. I didn't want the high school gossip mill to start grinding.

I want to talk with you, I thought to Hunter. *Please come.*

Hunter walked up to my car a few moments later. I leaned over and opened the passenger door, and he got in. "What is it?" he asked.

"I think that if you know your father's alive, then you ought to contact him."

Hunter stared out through the windshield. "You think so?"

"Yes," I said firmly. "I know it's not quite the same thing, but I only found out that I was adopted a couple of months ago. I'm still trying to find out what the truth is. It drives me crazy not to know. And with your dad—if you don't contact him, it will just eat at you. You'll never stop wondering."

"I've wondered about him every day for the last ten years," Hunter said. "Wondering is nothing new."

"What are you scared of?" I asked.

He gave me an annoyed glance. "What is it with this country? Are all Americans amateur shrinks? You've got therapists on the radio and therapists on the telly, and every one of you speaks fluent psychobabble."

Then he shut his eyes and rubbed them with one hand. I wanted to hold his other hand.

"I'm sorry," he said. He blew out a breath. "I miss England," he said. "I never feel right here. Being a witch and a Seeker on top of that already make me an outsider, but here everything feels *off*. I'm never at home."

I hadn't realized that, and the insight made me feel a strange, new tenderness for him. "I'm sorry," I said. "That must be awful."

"I'm getting used to it. I've even gotten used to you, your forthrightness." He gave me a rueful smile. "You hit close to the bone, Morgan, more often than you realize." He sighed. "It's probably good for me."

"Probably," I agreed. "Now, what about your father?"

"I don't know," he said. "It's loaded. Both in an emotional way—I'm terrified that since the message I got was only from him, it means my mother is dead—and in the sense that I don't know what effect my contacting him will have on the dark wave. I could be opening a Pandora's box that I'll never be able to close. I have to think about it."

"I—I shouldn't be so pushy. I don't know how you feel. Not really."

His hand closed over mine. "You were being a friend, and I have precious few of those. Thank you."

I loved how his hand felt on mine, then wondered how I could feel that way so soon after Cal. And then I told myself

I didn't owe Cal anything. Finally I decided it was too much for me to figure out, and I should just take what delight I could from the moment. "You're welcome," I said.

"It's late. I shouldn't keep you." Hunter took his hand away, and I felt a pang.

"It's okay," I said. I wanted so strongly to take his hand again that I actually slid my own hand under my thigh to keep it still.

He sounded exhausted. "We're still scheduled to work together tomorrow afternoon, right?"

I nodded. "I'm going to my aunt's house after church. I'll call you when I get home."

He got out of the car. "Get home safe, then." Hunter traced the rune Eolh in the air. "And sweet dreams."

19.
Pursuit

I'm going to contact my father.

I'm terribly afraid. Not just of putting him and Mum in danger, nor of putting myself in danger. More than that, I'm afraid of how changed he'll look, how old. I'm afraid he'll tell me Mum is dead. I'm afraid he'll tell me that he's heard I'm a Seeker, and he's ashamed of me.

I want to ask Morgan if she'll stay with me while I do it.

—Giomanach

I didn't sleep well that night. My mind was whirling with thoughts of Aunt Eileen and Paula, of finding the right spell to help them, of David, of Cal, of Hunter. I'd never been as confused about anyone as I was about Hunter. I bounced from thinking he was the most insufferable male on the planet to seeing, beneath all that arrogance, one of the most complex and fascinating people I'd ever met. There was no neat way to sum up Hunter Niall or my feelings about him.

The next morning I got up early again. I left a note for my family, saying I'd be back in time for church. Then I went for a drive. I needed to think, and I didn't want to be at home when I did. I bought myself coffee, then headed along the river to a small sailing marina.

The marina was dead quiet, since it was the middle of December. Most of the boats had been pulled into dry dock and rested on pilings in a fenced yard. I got out of the car with my cup of hot coffee and walked along the waterfront. The air was bitterly cold, but that was okay. It would force me to make my decision quickly.

What was I going to do about Aunt Eileen and Paula? Every instinct told me that I had the power to protect them, but I knew the charm I'd made wouldn't be enough. If I wanted to be sure that those thugs never bothered them again, I'd have to take more direct action. How dangerous was that?

The wind whipped off the river in an icy gust, and I decided on procrastination: I'd go visit Aunt Eileen and Paula and see if they were serious about leaving. If they were, then I'd try the spell I'd found last night on the Internet.

Shaking with cold, I got back into Das Boot.

I arrived at Aunt Eileen and Paula's just in time to see a police cruiser pulling away. Oh, no, I thought. I was too late. My heart racing with dread, I ran toward the house.

Aunt Eileen opened the door seconds after I rang the bell. "Morgan! What are you doing up this early on a Sunday? I thought you and Mary K. were coming by later."

"I—I was worried about you two," I said honestly. "I just saw the police car pulling away and—"

She smiled and put a comforting arm around me. "Come on in," she said. "Have some breakfast with us, and we'll tell you all about our undercover triumph."

"Your what?"

Paula was in the kitchen, cooking eggs, spinach, and mushrooms in a skillet. "Morgan!" she said. "Care for some breakfast?"

"Sure," I said, pulling up a chair. "Now, what happened?"

Aunt Eileen gave me a sheepish glance. "I felt like an idiot after I got off the phone with your sister yesterday. I was totally giving in to hysteria and fear."

"And to those jerks," Paula added. "For the record, I was equally hysterical."

"We decided we couldn't give in to them," Aunt Eileen continued.

Paula set down three plates containing eggs. "Short version: We drove to a security store in Kingston and rented a couple of surveillance cameras. Then we came home and put them up. At about two o'clock this morning, the camera at the back of the house caught our vandals on tape and sounded a little alarm in our bedroom. We called the cops. They were too late to catch the kids in the act, but they took the tape."

"The cruiser that just left," Eileen finished, "came to tell us that all three are now in custody, and one of them has confessed. The DA thinks she can charge them with at least two other local hate crimes. And two of them are old enough to be tried as adults. What's more, two of our neighbors on the block have offered to testify to what they saw. The community is being really supportive, I'm happy to say."

"Wow!" I exclaimed, amazed. "That's fabulous!" I nearly collapsed with relief. They had solved their own problem without my help, without magick. The choice had been taken out of my hands.

Aunt Eileen sighed. "I'm glad we caught those kids, but I have to say this whole incident has really shaken me. I mean, you hear about gay bashing all the time, but it's just not the same as when you're actually experiencing it. It's totally terrifying."

"I know," I agreed. Then I couldn't help asking anxiously, "But . . . you're not going to move?"

"Nope," Paula promised. "We've decided to tough it out here—at least for now. You can't solve this kind of problem by running away from it."

"That is the best news! I am so thrilled," I told them. I got up and opened the fridge. "Oh, no," I groaned.

"What?" Aunt Eileen sounded worried. "What's the matter?"

I turned from the fridge, which was full of disgustingly healthy foods. "Don't you guys have any Diet Coke?"

After breakfast with Paula and Aunt Eileen, I helped them rearrange living-room furniture; then I drove to church and met my family there. I made the effort because I wanted to make my parents happy—and because I felt badly in need of a nonmagickal, normal day.

After church the whole family opted out of our normal Widow's Vale Diner lunch so we could go back to Taunton for more unpacking. We got back to our house at three-thirty, and I decided to have a nice, long soak in the bathtub before calling Hunter.

The bath never happened. I'd just turned on the hot water faucet when I felt Hunter and Sky approaching. With a sigh I turned off the bathwater and went downstairs. Now what?

I opened the front door and waited. They both looked grim.

"Yes?" I demanded. "Aren't we scheduled to meet later?"

"This couldn't wait," he said.

"Come in." I led them into the den. After shutting the door I asked, "Is it Stuart Afton?"

"He's the same," Hunter answered. He looked at Sky. "Tell her."

"Last night," Sky began, "Bree and Raven and I were out studying the constellations by the old Methodist cemetery. We saw David. He was performing a ritual. A ritual I recognized."

"So what was it?" I asked.

Sky glanced at Hunter. Then she met my gaze steadily. "He was letting blood as a preliminary ritual to a larger sacrifice that will be performed once the moon moves into a different quarter."

"Bloodletting?" I said. I looked back and forth between Sky and Hunter.

"It's a payoff," Hunter said. "For services rendered. It fits with the ritual markings I found in the field where you had first felt a dark presence. He needs to offer his own blood to call in the taibhs, the dark spirit. Remember, that's how I knew it wasn't Selene. She has enough power to call a taibhs without performing that particular rite."

I felt sick. "Well, I guess that's the proof you were looking for, then," I said to Hunter.

"It's proof that he's using dark magick," Hunter said. "It

still doesn't connect him irrevocably to Stuart Afton. But that's just a formality now."

"David may not have bargained on or agreed to Stuart Afton having a stroke," Sky put in. "That's the kind of extra tithe that attaches itself when you deal with the blackness."

"In any case," Hunter said, "I've contacted the council, and they've told me to examine David formally."

There was something terrible in that sentence. "What does that mean?"

"It means that with the power vested in me by the council I am to ask David whether or not he's called on the dark energies," Hunter explained, not sounding like himself. "The procedure requires that two blood witches witness my examination of him."

I looked at him.

"It will be Sky and Alyce," he said, answering my unspoken question. "We're going to do it now, right away. There's no point in wasting any more time."

"I want to go, too," I said.

He shook his head, and Sky looked upset. "No. That's not necessary," he said. "I only came to tell you because I felt you needed to know."

"I'm coming," I said more strongly. "If David is innocent, that will come out in the examination. I want to be there to hear it. And if he's not . . ." I swallowed. "If he's not, I need to hear that, too."

Hunter and Sky looked at each other for a long moment, and I wondered if they were communicating telepathically. Finally Sky raised her eyebrows slightly. Hunter turned to me.

"You won't say anything, you won't do anything, you won't

interfere in any way," he said warningly. I raised my chin but didn't say a word. "If you do," he went on, "I'll put a binding spell on you that will make Cal's look like wet tissue paper."

"Let's go," I said.

We drove to Red Kill in Hunter's car. My stomach was tight with tension, and I kept swallowing. I felt cold and achy and full of dread. As much as I wanted Hunter to be wrong, all the evidence pointed to David.

When the three of us walked into Practical Magick, Alyce looked up. She looked tired and ill, her face drawn and almost gray. As soon as I saw her, I felt her pain over what was about to happen. She, too, believed David was guilty, I realized.

"We need David," Hunter said quietly.

David emerged from the back room. "I'm here," he said, his voice perfectly calm. "And I know why you're here."

"Will you come with us, then?" Hunter asked.

David glanced at Alyce and said, "Yes. Just let me get my jacket. Alyce, can you get the keys for the door?"

"Of course," she said.

David disappeared into the back room to get his jacket. And then didn't reappear. We waited maybe a minute and a half before Hunter tore behind the counter and into the back room. Sky and I followed. The door that led outside from the back room was ajar.

"Dammit!" Hunter swore, going through the door to a weedy, overgrown lot outside. "I didn't think he'd bolt. Stupid, stupid, stupid!"

I wasn't sure if he was referring to David or to himself, but I was too freaked out to ask. Sky was scanning the trees at the end of the lot. "He's in there," she told Hunter.

The two of them set off at a lope across the snow-patched ground, and I followed, sick at heart. Alyce, wrapped in a lavender shawl, bustled after us.

It was dark and shadowy inside the area of evergreens where David had disappeared. The trees were tall enough to block out most of the fading daylight, and we found ourselves in a murky gray light, peering around shadowy trunks for any sign of David. I cast my senses and felt Sky, Alyce, and Hunter doing the same. It was strange to feel my power joined to theirs in this way.

My senses picked up hibernating animals, a few birds. Was Sky wrong? Had David come in here? Or was he somehow masking himself?

Sky suddenly whirled. "There!" she cried as a ball of witch fire flew straight toward Hunter.

Hunter raised a hand and murmured something, and the witch fire was deflected, bouncing away from an invisible shield and landing in a snowbank with a sizzle.

It seemed the witch fire had come from behind a tall blue spruce. Hunter moved toward it with a predator's quiet intensity.

Another ball of witch fire sped toward him, which he brushed off, not even bothering with the charm this time. I realized something in Hunter had changed. It was as if he was drawing power into him, taking in energies far beyond his own considerable powers, linked to the life force all around us. But it was even more than that.

Hearing my silent question, Sky said, "When he acts as Seeker, he can draw on the power of others on the council."

God, how much else did I not know? "Will the extra power protect him?"

"Yes and no. The act of drawing power itself will wear him out if he tries to use it for too long. But it will help him fight certain kinds of attacks."

"David Redstone of Clan Burnhide, I summon you to answer to the International Council of Witches. Athar of Kithic and Alyce of Starlocket appear as witnesses," Hunter stated in a cold, relentless voice. "You will stand forth now."

I heard David make a strange sound, as if he were in pain, and I wondered about the power of Hunter's words.

"Stand forth now!" Hunter repeated.

David staggered forward from behind the spruce, his eyes wild, pure animal terror driving him now.

The sapphire in Hunter's athame glowed with power. I watched as he traced a rectangle of blue light around David's body. David screamed and doubled over, trapped in the blue light. Hunter moved in quickly, and I saw the deceptively delicate silver chain, the braigh, appear in his hand.

Alyce put her hand to her mouth, her eyes full of anguish.

I couldn't watch but buried my face in Sky's shoulder as Hunter wrapped the silver chain around David's wrists. I heard David screaming and remembered Cal writhing in agony as Hunter bound his wrists.

"Let me go!" David was shouting. "I did nothing wrong!"

I opened my eyes. David was on his knees in the snow, his wrists bound by the silver chain. The flesh around the chain was already raised in angry red welts. Tears streamed from his eyes.

Hunter stood over him, stern and unyielding. "Tell us the

truth," he said. "Did you summon a taibhs to get Stuart Afton to forgive your aunt's debt?"

"I did it for the people who lived above the store," David insisted. "They would have been homeless."

Hunter pulled on the braigh, and David screamed in agony.

"Yes," David sobbed. "I made offerings to the taibhs in exchange for its help."

"Did you offer it Stuart Afton's life?"

"No, never!" Hunter pulled on the braigh again, but David didn't change his answer. "I just asked the taibhs to make him change his mind," he said. "I never wanted harm to come to him. I deliberately asked that no harm be done to anyone when I cast the spell."

"That was foolish." Hunter's voice was surprisingly gentle. "Don't you know that's the one request the blackness will never grant? It feeds on destruction, and all who seek out the darkness are powerless to control it."

David was sobbing.

Hunter turned to look at us. "Alyce of Starlocket, do you need to hear more?"

"No," Alyce choked out, weeping silently.

"Athar of Kithic? Are you convinced?"

"Yes," Sky said in an almost whisper.

Hunter looked at me then, an unspoken question in his eyes. I didn't answer, but my own tears were answer enough.

Hunter nodded and knelt next to David. I was surprised to see him put a hand on David's back and help him stand. Hunter seemed sad, tired, and old beyond his years. "Sky and I will take David to our house for safekeeping," he said quietly. "The council will decide what to do."

20.
Dark and Bright

I put the braigh on David Redstone today. Morgan was there. She saw the whole thing. I doubt she'll ever forgive me.

But I have to make her try, because I need her. Goddess, how I need her.

I think I'm falling in love. And I'm frightened.

—Giomanach

Seeing David standing there in the snowy woods, tortured and ashamed, seeing the pain in Hunter's face caused by doing his job, made something snap in me. Without realizing what I was doing, I bolted. As I ran, I stumbled in the snow. Branches caught at my clothes. A birch twig tangled itself in my hair. I ran on, feeling my hair pull, hearing the snap of the twig. The tree flashed a current of pain. Everything that was alive was hurting, and I was part of the web, hurting and in turn causing pain.

I broke out of the woods and found myself behind an office building, its windows dark. Practical Magick was nowhere in sight. I had no idea where I was, and I didn't care. I kept running, my toes numb in my boots as they hit the tarmac. I was panting, my breath short, my chest aching. Then there were footsteps and a familiar presence behind me. Sky.

"Morgan, please stop!" she shouted.

I wondered if I could outrun her and realized that I was too worn out to try. I slowed to a walk, my heart pounding, and let her catch up with me.

She was panting, too. She waited until her breathing slowed before saying, "A formal questioning by a Seeker is never easy to witness."

"Easy?" I nearly shrieked. "I would have settled for non-horrific. I can't believe that Hunter *chooses* to do that."

Sky's jaw literally dropped. "Do you think he enjoyed that?"

I was still repulsed and sickened by what I'd seen. "He chose it," I said. "Hunter became a Seeker, knowing what he would be required to do. He's *good* at it."

There was long beat of silence, and then Sky said, "I'd slap you silly if I thought you knew what you were talking about."

Before I knew what I was doing I had shot out my hand, spinning off a ball of witch fire. Instantly Sky held up a finger, and the fire fizzled out like a Fourth of July sparkler.

"You're not the only blood witch here," she told me in a low, angry voice. "And while you may have more innate power than any witch I've seen, I've had a great deal more practice working it. So don't turn this into a fight, because you won't win."

I hadn't meant to send the witch fire at her. I was just so

angry and sickened and exhausted that her threat was enough to make something inside me lash out. "I'm too tired to fight," I said.

"Fine, then get over yourself and listen for a minute. What Hunter does is harder on him that it is on anyone else."

"Then why does he do it?" I choked out the question. "Why?"

Sky thrust her hands into the pockets of her jacket. "In large part because of Linden's death. He still feels responsible. Being a Seeker is Hunter's atonement. He feels that if he can protect others from courting the dark, then maybe his brother's death won't be in vain. But it eats him alive whenever he has to do something like what he did to David."

The wind picked up, and I pulled my collar higher. "It sounds like he's punishing himself."

"I believe that's true," she admitted. "Even though the council acquitted him of all responsibility in Linden's death. Hunter's like a pit bull. He doesn't let go of anything—not the good or the bad. He'll be loyal to the death, but he'll also carry every grief with him to the grave."

We were drawing closer to another strip mall. There were neon lights, cars, people hurrying into stores. It seemed so strange that the normal world existed so close to the woods where David had been just bound by an ancient and terrible magick.

"I still don't see how Hunter can stand to be a Seeker," I said. "It's as if he's chosen to always be miserable."

Sky turned to face me. "There's another way to look at it, you know. Hunter's seen the destruction and grief caused by the dark side, and he's dedicated his life to fighting it. He's fighting the good fight, Morgan. How can you hate him for that?"

"I can't," I said quietly. "I don't."

"There's something else," she went on. "As the only surviving descendent of Belwicket, you must realize how vital it is that you help him in this fight. We can't let the dark wave win."

I shook my head, feeling dazed. "I thought I was finally okay with all of this—being a blood witch, being adopted, even dealing with Cal and what he did to me. Now there's this war against the dark side, too."

"Yes," Sky said. "And it's as dreadful and painful as any war ever fought. I'm sorry you're caught in it."

"My family doesn't even know the dark side exists."

"I wouldn't say that. They're Catholics, aren't they? The Church has a pretty well-defined notion of evil. They just give it different names than we do and use different means to deal with it. Darkness and evil have always been part of the world, Morgan."

"And I just lucked into getting close to it?"

Sky smiled. "Something like that. The only comfort is knowing you're not alone in the fight." She nodded toward a phone booth at the end of the strip mall. "I told Hunter to take David home. We'd better call someone if we're ever going to get home from here. How about Bree?"

I dug some change out of my pocket. "I'll call her."

Bree came and got us and drove us home. I went to sleep at once, and the next day I lay low at school. I avoided everyone in the coven, even avoided friends who weren't part of my Wiccan life. I was aching everywhere. I felt beaten, hurt, betrayed by my own birthright. I couldn't help thinking of that first circle with Cal. Wicca had been so beautiful to me. Now it was wound through with pain.

After school I drove Mary K. home and immediately shut myself in my room to do homework—calculus and history and English, all of it reassuringly mundane. I wanted nothing to do with magick. Mary K. poked her head in at one point, told me she was going out with her friend Darcy and that she'd be home in time for dinner.

It was my turn to cook, so at five-thirty I went down to the kitchen and started rummaging through the pantry and freezer. I found some ground beef, onions, canned tomatoes, garlic, a can of mild green chiles, and a box of cornbread mix.

I was putting diced onions into the cast-iron skillet when I sensed Hunter's presence. Dammit, I thought, what do you want now? Resigned, I turned off the flame beneath the pan.

Hunter was coming up the walk when I opened the door. He looked drained.

"I'm making dinner," I said. I turned around and went into the kitchen. I knew he was hurting, but I couldn't bring myself to even look at him. Despite what Sky had told me, despite what I knew in my own heart, all I could see right now was the Seeker.

He followed me into the kitchen. I turned the burner back on beneath the skillet and started chopping up the tomatoes.

"I came to see if you were all right," Hunter said. "I know yesterday was rough on you."

"It doesn't look like it was great for you, either." He moved as if he were badly beaten up.

"It's always hard," he said in a low voice. "And I didn't manage to deflect all the witch fire he shot at me."

I was surprised to realize how much the thought of him being hurt scared me. "Are you all right?" I asked.

"I'll heal."

I added the chilies and tomatoes to the pan and poured the cornbread mix into a bowl.

"I've got bad news," Hunter said. "I've heard from the council. They've passed sentence on David."

I dropped the wooden spoon I was holding. Hunter reached for it in the same instant that I did. He caught it and handed it to me.

"David must be bound and his magick stripped from him." Hunter's jaw trembled as he spoke, and I knew with certainty that this was harder on him than on anyone, except maybe, in this case, David. David had once told me that witches can lose their minds if they can't practice magick.

"So the council strips him?" I asked.

Hunter's face looked harsh beneath the kitchen's fluorescents. "I do. Tomorrow at sunset at my house. I'll need witnesses. Four of them—blood witches."

I stared at him, seeing the pain on his face, and knew what he wanted to ask me.

"No," I said, backing away from him. "You can't ask me to be part of that."

"Morgan," he said gently.

Suddenly I was crying, unable to hold it back anymore. "I hate this," I sobbed. "I hate it if having magick means I have to be part of this. I never asked for this. I'm tired and I hurt and I don't want to hurt anymore."

"I know," Hunter told me, his own voice breaking. His arms wrapped around me, and I let myself fall onto his chest. When I looked up, I saw that his eyes were wet with tears. "I'm so sorry, Morgan."

At that moment I remembered something Cal had told me: that there is beauty and darkness in everything. Sorrow in joy, life in death, thorns on the rose. I knew then that I could not escape pain and torment any more than I could give up joy and beauty.

I clung to Hunter, sobbing, in the middle of my kitchen. He murmured nonsense words and stroked my hair gently. Finally my sobs quieted, and I pulled away. Wiping my eyes, I turned the heat off under the frying pan before it all burned.

Hunter drew a deep breath and brushed a tear from my cheek. "Look at us. Two kick-ass witches falling to pieces."

I reached for a tissue on the counter and blew my nose. "I must look like hell."

"No. You look like someone who has the courage to face even what breaks your heart, and I find you . . . beautiful."

Then his mouth found mine and we were kissing. At first the kiss was gentle, reassuring, but then something in me took over, and I pressed against him with an urgency and intensity that shook us both. It was as though there was something in Hunter I wanted with a hunger I barely recognized—something in him I needed the way I needed air to breathe. And clearly he felt that way, too.

When we pulled back, my mouth felt swollen, my eyes huge. "Oh," I said.

"Oh, indeed," he said softly.

We stood there for a long moment, looking at each

other as if we were seeing each other for the first time. My heart was beating like crazy, and I was wondering what to say when I heard my dad's car pulling into the driveway.

"Well." Hunter ran a hand through his hair. "I'd better go."

"Yes."

I walked him to the door, and suddenly the reason for his visit came rushing back. "Tomorrow is going to be terrible, isn't it?" I said.

"Yes." He waited, not looking at me.

"All right." I leaned my head against the door frame. "I'll be there." I wanted to cry again, and I said, "Oh, Goddess, is anything ever going to feel good again?"

"Yes." Hunter kissed me again, quickly. "It will. I promise. But not until after tomorrow."

On Tuesday at sunset we gathered at Hunter and Sky's house for the ceremony. Sky and Hunter were there, of course, and so was a skinny teenage boy who looked familiar. "Where do I know you from?" I asked him.

"Probably from the party at Practical Magick. I play guitar with The Fianna. That was a sweet night," he said sadly.

"You're Alyce's nephew."

He nodded and held out his hand. "Diarmuid." He shifted uneasily. "Lousy occasion to be formally introduced."

"Will Alyce be here?" I asked.

"Already is," he said in a grim tone. "She started crying the moment we walked through the door. She's upstairs with Sky now. Auntie Alyce always wants to believe the best of everyone. She still can't quite believe it—that David called on the dark side. He's her dear friend, you know."

When everyone had assembled, there were five of us in the living room: Hunter, Sky, Alyce, Diarmuid, and me. Wordlessly Hunter led us to the room at the back of the house.

Candles flickered on the altar and in each of the four corners of the room. Outside, wind swept through the ravine, sending a high keening sound into the room.

David knelt in the very center of the room, inside a pentagram of glowing sapphire light. He wore a simple white shirt and white pants. He was barefoot. His hands were bound behind him with rope, his head bowed. He looked fragile and frightened. I ached to hold him, to comfort him somehow. But I knew I couldn't get past the light.

Hunter gestured, and we each stood on one point of the pentagram, with Hunter at the top of it. I noticed a drum on the floor behind Sky. Alyce stood quietly, her eyes locked on David and filled with grief.

Hunter surrounded the pentagram in a circle of salt, tracing signs for each of the four directions and invoking the Guardian of each.

"We call on the Goddess and the God," he began, "to be with us in this rite of justice. With the setting of the sun we take from David Redstone the magick that you gifted him.

"No more shall he wake a witch. No more shall he know your beauty or your power. No more shall he do harm. No more shall he be one of us.

"David Redstone, the International Council of Witches has met and passed judgment on you," Hunter went on in a still, neutral voice. "You called on a dark spirit, and as a result a man nearly died. For that you are to be punished by having your powers stripped from you. Do you understand?"

David lifted his head and nodded. His eyes were shut, as though he couldn't bear to keep them open.

"You must answer," Hunter said. "Do you understand the punishment that is now passed on you?"

"Yes." David's voice was barely audible.

Alyce bit back a cry of dismay, and I saw Diarmuid grasp her hand.

"Anger has no place here," Hunter cautioned us. "We are here for justice, not vengeance. Let us begin."

Sky began to beat a slow, solemn rhythm on the drum. The drumbeats seemed to go on forever. Gradually I noticed something shifting in the room. The drum was guiding us, subtly working on each one of us so that our breath aligned with it, our pulses followed it, and our energy joined and began to travel along the sapphire blue light of the pentagram as a line of blazing white.

I saw David hunch in on himself, as if trying to make himself small so that neither the blue light nor the white light could touch him.

The drum beat faster, more insistently, and the light intensified. The energy of five blood witches was fully intertwined now. The energy flowing around the pentagram crackled with power. We all held out our hands, drawing on the power, and I almost wept to feel my energy pouring out, familiar and strong.

Hunter stepped forward and touched the hilt of his athame to the pentagram. For a second the knife lit with blue and white light. The light continued to define the pentagram, but now Hunter walked around it, drawing his athame in a spiral around David, and the sapphire and white light blazed in a spiral as well.

I watched as our power flowed into the spiral and the spiral began to whirl around David. He whimpered as a transparent, smokelike image of a boy I recognized as himself appeared and vanished on the whirls of the spiral. Next came images of David in his robe, athame in hand, casting spells; David finding a wounded bird, making the sign of a healing rune over it and watching in delight as the bird flew from his hand; David charting the phases of the moon and its effect on the tides; David scrying with a crystal; David purifying Practical Magick with cedar and sage; David and another man facing each other in a circle and chanting in perfect harmony. All of it was leaving him, flying up the spiral like escaping spirits. And with each thing that left him, he sobbed with grief, a man watching everything he loved being destroyed. These were the experiences that had shaped him, that he used to define himself. They had formed the fabric of his life, and we were unraveling it.

When the very last of David's magick had vanished on the whirls of the spiral, Hunter held out the hilt of his athame, drawing the glowing spiral into it once again.

"David Redstone, witch of the Burnhides, is now ended," Hunter said gently. "The Goddess teaches us that every ending is also a beginning. May there be rebirth from this death."

The drumbeat finally stopped, and with it the sapphire light of the pentagram winked out. David lay collapsed on the floor, a hollow shell. I wanted to fall over, too, but I stayed upright, feeling if I moved, I would crack into a million brittle pieces.

Alyce bent down slowly and put her arms around David.

"Goddess be with you," she murmured; then Diarmuid had to lead her out because she was weeping uncontrollably.

Sky watched silent and stricken as Hunter cut the bonds on David's wrists and gently helped him to his feet. "I'm going to give you some herbs to help you sleep," Hunter told David. The stern Seeker was gone from Hunter now, and he seemed only tender and sad. "Come with me," he said, taking David by the hand.

David let himself be led, walking with halting steps, like a lost child in a man's body.

Sky ran her hand through her hair and blew out a breath. "Are you all right?" she asked me as they left the room.

"It wasn't what I expected," I said. "I thought it would be more like the braigh."

"You mean, physical torture?"

I nodded. "This was gentler. And yet, much worse." I thought of how Selene had wanted to take my power for herself. Goddess, what would that have been like? It was unthinkable.

"I never want to do anything like it again." Sky walked to each corner of the room and extinguished the candles there but left the two on the altar lit. "Let's get out of here," she said with a shudder. "I'll come back in and do a purification ceremony in the morning."

Moving in slow motion, I followed her into the living room.

"We found out what happened, you know," Sky said. "The taibhs terrified Afton so badly that he wanted nothing to do with the store. That's why he forgave the debt. Then, later, the continued stress of the encounter led to the stroke. Receiving Alyce's muffins was what pushed him over the edge."

"You mean Alyce . . ." It was unbelievable.

"She had sent them as a thank-you. But dark forces work in devious ways, and so her kindness resulted in a terrible event." Sky put a finger to her lips. "She doesn't know, and I hope you won't tell her. It would hurt her too much."

I nodded. Then a thought occurred to me. "What happens to the store now?"

"Hunter spoke with Afton. He's getting better, but he wants nothing to do with Practical Magick. And the bookstore deal fell through, so the building has lost its value." Sky shrugged. "I think Alyce will probably have to pay off the debt, but Afton seems willing to work with her on the timing. She'll be able to keep the store running." She touched my shoulder comfortingly, and left the room.

I heard Hunter coming down the stairs and turned to look at him. "Morgan," he said. "You're still here." He looked exhausted and so much older than he had earlier that day. He came to stand before me. "Thank you. I know how hard that was for you."

I looked at him. He wasn't a monster. He had done what he had to, and through it all there'd been an undercurrent of compassion streaming from him, from Hunter to all of us.

"I have something for you." He reached into his pocket and took out a clear, faceted crystal.

"Quartz?" I guessed.

He gave me a look that made it clear that was the wrong answer.

"Oh, Hunter, please, I'm too worn out for guessing games."

"Tell me what it is," he said softly.

So I tried, thinking of the stones I'd learned, trying to fit a name to it: Zircon? Danburite? Diamond? Albite? It couldn't be moonstone. Frustrated, I sent my energy into the stone, asking it to yield its name to me. The answer it gave made no sense.

I gazed up at Hunter, baffled. "What it tells me is beryl, but that can't be right. Beryl is either aquamarine or emerald, and this is—"

"Morganite," he told me. "Your name stone, another form of beryl."

"Morganite?"

"It changes colors with the sunlight. At different times of day it will be white, lavender, pink, even pale blue. It's a powerful healing stone. And there's something else it can do." His hand closed around the stone. He looked at me, and his green eyes were as fathomless as the sea. "If a blood witch holds it and sends energy into it, it will reveal what is deepest in his heart."

Hunter opened his hand, and in the very center of the crystal I saw myself.